What the critics are saying...

"FELIDAE is an intriguing and unique concept that I found thoroughly engaging." ~ *Enya Adrian Romance Reviews Today*

"What do you get when you mix shape-shifters, ancient curses/spells, cats and hot sex? A very entertaining story." ~ *Sarah Silversmith The Romance Readers Connection*

"I could not put this book down; it kept me turning the pages. This book is a must read. You will not be disappointed." ~ *Dianne Nogueras eCataRomance*

"Paranormal twists and turns in it and the sex was HOT, HOT, HOT. If you like Paranormal/shape shifter romance then go to get this story, you will not regret it." ~ *Nicole Enchanted In Romance*

"Ciarra Sims weaves a sexy tale that reads like a mystery novel. And she has created an impressive backstory for her cat people with a history rich in cultural detail." ~ *Thor the Barbarian Thor the Barbarian Chronicles*

Felidae draws you into a world of shape-shifters, ancient spells, cats and luscious sex. Ciarra Sims's Felidae is a story I would recommend as a read for any reader that is looking for a wonderful tale of spicy passion and fun." ~ *M. Jeffers The Road to Romance*

"Ms. Sims has written a fabulous story for her reader's. I wasn't disappointed; check this book out it's great!" ~ *Susan Holly Just Erotic Romance Reviews*

"Felidae is innovative, sexy and purrrrrfectly delightful." ~ *Sarma Burdeu eCataRomance*

"Ms. Sims creates interesting plot twists and a suspenseful page-turner that held me captive to the last page. There is no doubt this book is one to keep." ~ *Lindsey Ann Denson Karen Find Out About New Books Coffee Time Romance*

"This is a fun short novel which not only has very hot love scenes, but also makes you laugh. Throw in some shapeshifting, and some magic potions, blend well with skilled writing and a fast pace, and you have a great recipe for an amusing story." *Jean Fallen Angel Reviews*

CIARRA SIMS

FELINAE

ELLORA'S CAVE
ROMANTICA PUBLISHING

An Ellora's Cave Romantica Publication

www.ellorascave.com

Felidae

ISBN #1419952064
ALL RIGHTS RESERVED.
Felidae Copyright© 2004 Ciarra Sims
Edited by: Pamela Cohen
Cover art by: Syneca

Electronic book Publication: August, 2004
Trade paperback Publication: October, 2005

Excerpt from *The Phallas From Dallas*
Copyright © Ciarra Sims, 2003
Excerpt from *Walk on the Wild Side*
Copyright © Ciarra Sims, 2003

Warning:

The following material contains graphic sexual content meant for mature readers. *Felidae* has been rated *E-rotic* by a minimum of three independent reviewers.

Ellora's Cave Publishing offers three levels of Romantica™ reading entertainment: S (S-ensuous), E (E-rotic), and X (X-treme).

S-*ensuous* love scenes are explicit and leave nothing to the imagination.

E-*rotic* love scenes are explicit, leave nothing to the imagination, and are high in volume per the overall word count. In addition, some E-rated titles might contain fantasy material that some readers find objectionable, such as bondage, submission, same sex encounters, forced seductions, etc. E-rated titles are the most graphic titles we carry; it is common, for instance, for an author to use words such as "fucking", "cock", "pussy", etc., within their work of literature.

X-*treme* titles differ from E-rated titles only in plot premise and storyline execution. Unlike E-rated titles, stories designated with the letter X tend to contain controversial subject matter not for the faint of heart.

Also by Ciarra Sims:

The Phallus from Dallas
Walk on the Wild Side

Felidae

Dedication

To my mom for putting up with my idiosyncrasies all these years. And to Chippy, Morrie, Tia and Chelsea for teaching me the meaning of feline.

Prologue
Egypt 30 BC
The Beginning

Kiya was cresting the slight rise leading from the river when she heard the creak of leather and the muted clang of metal, as if someone trying to be stealthy had failed.

The water urn she carried was heavy, and the precious liquid sloshed and soaked her ankles as she fought the loosely packed sand to gain the summit and vantage point overlooking Meneion. The compact city was usually a picturesque example of tranquility and harmony this time of day. The field laborers could be seen in the distance threshing wheat, chanting rhythmically in low melodic tones, the sound reassuring to the otherwise sleepy city. An occasional sound of a cough or laughter could be heard coming from the various temples and domiciles.

Kiya was out on this hot afternoon to fetch enough water for her mistress' demanding tastes. Nitetis was the wife of a very important nobleman and advisor to the Queen. She treated Kiya just as she was…a slave. Pretty Kiya was old enough to be married, but her mistress forbade it of her slaves and therefore Kiya faced a life of servitude and nothing more. Nitetis was a hard mistress. Kiya's back bore the evidence of this. The fresh rushes that Nitetis used as whipping tools, hurt like fire, but left no deep scars. Kiya had received her latest beating only hours before when she had dropped a jug of water as she filled a shallow basin used to dampen a cloth to soothe her mistress' brow. But it was her lot and she accepted her place in the city's caste system.

Therefore, when Kiya glanced at the sandy hills surrounding Meneion and saw the lines of Roman soldiers sitting like impatient carrion birds, waiting to swoop down and commit carnage, she let out a cry of horror and warning. At the same moment a Roman General raised his lance and signaled for the charge. Kiya could only watch in horror as hundreds upon hundreds of the soldiers swarmed over the city.

The field laborers did what they could, but their scythes were no match for trained killers and they soon lay in heaps, their bodies cleaved and stabbed into final submission. The rest of the city became alive with the cries of surprised citizens awakened from their noonday sleep or were partaking in light meals. No one was given the chance to surrender. No one would survive.

For Meneion had received the Roman demand for subjugation weeks earlier. They had scoffed at the rumor of the soldiers who threatened to claim one city after another. Meneion's citizens were arrogant enough to believe they could withstand the Romans. Their gods would never allow the interlopers to have the upper hand. The most able-bodied, important men were attending a quorum to decide how best to fend off the marauding intruders. Days away, they would return to find the city burned, in ruins, and their wives and children slain. Not to mention, the laborers and fields destroyed. The city would perish.

Kiya could only watch helplessly as soldiers rode on armor-protected horses, and lanced fleeing unarmed Meneion citizens. They showed no mercy and killed without remorse. A woman carrying a baby dashed from her home, her legs no match for a soldier's war steed. He wasted not even a lance as he ran her down, trampling her and the baby beneath sharp hooves.

It did not take long. In an amazingly short time the sound of havoc ceased. Only the sound of the wounded and cries of the bereaved echoed down the streets and across the hill to where Kiya stood in shock. Even those noises were soon silenced by harsh means, as foot soldiers dispatched the wounded and looted the city, emptying the amply stocked coffers, and ferreting out any that tried to hide.

A girl no older than Kiya was dragged forth to the fountain in the town square. How beautiful the water was, the sun shining on its depths, reflecting like fine sparkling jewels. Kiya always loved the fountain. It had been a constant source of comforting calm in her otherwise mundane, repetitive life.

But today Kiya could only watch stunned as the girl's loose gown was torn, bodice to knees, and a soldier stripped off his light armor before lifting his own garment to expose his lower torso. Kiya had never seen a man's organ, though she knew by the other servants' talk and whispers what a man did to a woman. Her mistress forbade the act of love and so Kiya had never given it much thought, knowing the penalty for such willful disobedience would be far worse than a thrashing. Therefore, she would remain a maiden all her life, serving her mistress 'til the day one of them died.

But now as she watched the soldier mount the girl and jab his swollen flesh into her, Kiya realized Nitetis was probably dead and without her protection, such a thing was very likely to happen to her.

The distance made it hard to tell what else was happening, but the girl's cries were enough that Kiya knew she was in pain and frightened. No doubt she was a poor servant girl, an untried maiden, much like Kiya.

When the soldier climbed off, another took his place and another. Each mounted the girl like a rutting bull, his loins heaving against hers in a frenzy of vengeful copulation. The girl grew silent and when the soldiers were done, one casually drew a knife from the sheath at his side, and slit the despondent girl's throat, throwing her body into the fountain. The stain of inky blood spread throughout the water and even at that distance Kiya could see the water turning as red as an angry sun in a sandstorm. She thought she would never forget the sight as long as she lived. The town square littered with bodies, the fountain running with blood and the soldiers standing uncaring, not even bothering to pull down their garments, leaving their shriveled manhoods dangling limply without shame.

The shock of the events was wearing off and Kiya's trembling knees gave way. She dropped, sitting in a stupor on the crest of the rise. The movement drew a soldier's eye and he pointed upward in her direction. Another soldier laughed and made a lewd gesture with his hips, simulating what he had done to the servant girl. The three men turned as one and headed towards the rise where she slumped.

Kiya's heart pounded and her hands gripped the sand, feeling the sun-scorched granules burn her palms. The sudden pain brought back her senses. The soldiers were fast gaining the rise. Kiya leapt to her feet and took off down the slope towards the river. The soldiers quickened their pace and Kiya knew she had little chance without stealth and luck.

She headed for the shifting dunes, where the sand was deep and the soldiers might flounder. She herself knew this land, just as she knew her place in it, and with that knowledge came the certainty the fickle dunes were her salvation. She pumped her short, stocky legs and drew breath as she approached the hilly, bare dunes. A half-mile of silt and sand, they shifted at whim and the wind could change them overnight.

Kiya ran until her lungs felt they would burst. She raced in a choppy, sprinting gait, heel first, to gain headway. The dunes rose and fell in a sea of sand, consistently ascending in stair-step fashion, as if leading to heaven.

Daring to look back, Kiya saw the soldiers trying to climb, their sandal toes sinking deep as they scrabbled to keep their balance. Overcome by emotion, Kiya turned and in her native tongue yelled, "I curse you! You are murderers and thieves and I curse you into the afterlife. Know this and rot in your tombs like the rat vermin you are!"

One of the soldiers must have understood as he hurled back words. "Pretty speech for a girl about to feel my staff and my blade within her. Run, my pretty Egyptian harlot, run! The gutting of the prey is so much more exhilarating after a chase." He found his foothold and began to climb.

Kiya trembled and took off. Her passionate outcry about tombs formed as an idea. The Valley of the Dead was on the other side of the dunes. For centuries, kings and honored noblemen had been buried and entombed in great pyramids and vaults; their possessions and favorite animals and servants buried within, to sustain them in the afterlife. Perhaps Kiya could find shelter in the valley, or gain divine guidance by praying to the gods at one of the temples erected for such a purpose.

By the time Kiya reached the last dune bordering the valley, she was worn out. The Roman soldiers must be in the lower dip of a dune, still headed her way. When she looked back, before entering the steep slope down into the Valley of the Dead, she could see nothing behind her. But she could sense the danger. And it was close.

It was rumored the valley held great healing powers, and if one could gain the protection of its interior, they could be cured of affliction. This would not have been such a lofty goal to obtain, except the sickly or maimed had to venture into the valley on their own momentum and bring a sacrifice, or at minimum, an offering to appease the gods. Anything less would have been deemed an insult, payable by self-sacrifice as forfeit.

Even healthy, Kiya was having a hard time of it, as she scrabbled for a hold to ease down the steep embankment into the valley. The sand was transformed into pure rock, slippery and loosely covered with temperamental granules that rolled unstably under her feet. She slipped countless times and grasped for holds, her nails chipping away and bleeding as she slid gracelessly.

Halfway down she turned to look up, checking on her progress and the Romans. It was her downfall as her thin-soled already worn-through slippers slid out from under her and she pitched forward. The descent was a mix of a roll and a slide, Kiya's arms flailing helplessly, unable to stop the momentum. She reached the bottom and hit hard. She groaned and lay quietly. Above she heard voices.

Kiya forced her eyes open and ignored the shooting pain through her body and the stab in her wrist. A sharp rock had opened a deep cut and blood flowed freely. She tried to stanch the wound with the hemline of the light blue tunic she wore. But, it was ridiculously apparent as she daubed at the slash in her wrist and the blood ran in rivulets, the effort was futile. The cut was too deep.

There was no time to further worry on her injury. Death came in many forms and the ones above were foremost on her mind. To punctuate these thoughts, rocks from above began rolling around her, bouncing off the face of the valley wall as the soldiers began their dogged descent.

Kiya forced herself to her feet and half-raced, half-hobbled down the valley floor. In front of her stood the awe-inspiring daunting pyramids that invoked reverent approach and silence. But Kiya could not take the chance of slowing and prayed her ancestors would not take offense. She approached the tomb of Ahhotep and bowed her head humbly as she raced by. She hoped to lose herself somewhere in the middle of the tombs. The vast size of these death temples made her bow down, afraid lest she waken spirits long dead and at rest.

The second tomb was smaller, signifying a Prince. It was Ahhotep's son. All around were smaller vaults where revered noblemen had been buried, but these held no sanctuary for a living body. Then twin pyramids jutted to the sky and Kiya darted between these, her head swiveling back and forth, looking furtively for somewhere she could hide. The temples set up outside these monstrosities of stone blocks were small in comparison to the tombs. They were simple one-room buildings holding an altar for offerings, beads, jewels, or food. They offered no shelter and Kiya could not hope for asylum, as no one attended these shrines. The worshipping and personal sacrifices were a sacred, private affair and not to be witnessed by others.

Kiya felt blood from her wrist spattering her feet as she hobbled on between the rows of sun-scorched blocks, piled high into the sky. The geometric shapes were so perfect it was as if the gods themselves had a hand in their creation.

The last pyramid in the valley was the largest. Kiya had not meant to go this far. She did not want to approach Taharqa's final resting place. It was rumored Taharqa still walked the valley on moonless nights, restless over his brutal murder by his wife and her lover, Taharqa's very own brother, who usurped the throne after his death.

Legend said Taharqa cursed his brother and vowed he would invoke the gods to seek vengeance not only on him, but also his progeny, until the line died out. Even if it meant walking as a creature of the night for eternity and never claiming his place in the after world, Taharqa vowed to take his revenge.

It was said Taharqa was made a god of vengeance and betrayal and demanded a high price for his summoning. The pyramid itself was dark, quarried of black stone that cast a funereal shadow over the end of the valley. Kiya could not help the shiver that coursed through her body as she stood in the dark pall where the sun could not reach, contemplating the sacrilege she was about to commit.

Taharqa's temple was a dark affair of the same black stone as his pyramidal tomb. It never wore or chipped, as did the other temples and pyramids, despite the gale force winds and sandstorms that could shred a human's skin to ribbons, and blew through the valley without warning.

The temple had stood for centuries, alongside the pyramid, somber and brooding. Two obelisks signaled the entrance, but did not offer succor.

The twin tower-like structures stood guard and dared interlopers to breach their confines and cross the threshold into the temple's darkness. Unlike the other temples in the valley, Taharqa's was composed of only one room with no courtyard to encourage tranquil composure before entering the hall of worship, no simple shrine to make an offering of material goods.

Instead, the black temple was a cavern, backing up to the pyramid. The only offerings Taharqa received were sacrifices, as few souls had the courage to approach the ebony pyramid, and only the most desperate dared to. If the sacrifice were not worthy, legend said the dark pyramid's inhabitant would devour the offerer in its place. Since one could never be sure which sacrifices would be deemed worthy, the ritual sacrifices to Taharqa had stopped a few centuries past.

The sound of the Romans' voices bounced around the valley, making it hard for Kiya to judge where they came from and how close. She looked anxiously at the entrance to the Temple of Taharqa and quivered in fear. But her head swam and she knew she had to find a place to hide quickly. She crept inside the temple and the darkness swallowed her. Could she remain here undetected? The light blue tunic she wore was a danger in itself, as it showed even in the darkness. Without hesitation Kiya disrobed and threw the tunic behind the strange altar that rose up in the middle of the room. From somewhere above, a weak shaft of light shone down onto the black slab of stone that waited solemnly for its next blood offering.

Kiya thought she might indeed be safe and breathed deep before exhaling her ragged breath. Just to be certain she crept forward and in the near black of the temple, approached the altar. "Oh, Great Taharqa, I apologize for breaching your dark world and disturbing your rest. Please forgive me and take my humble offering. It is all I have in the world." Kiya reached up to her neck. Her fingers were sticky and she realized the blood from her wrist wound was thickening as it slowed. The gold collar she wore that symbolized her stature as a servant from the house of Ramboul was hard to take off. It was suppose to be forged in place, but last week Kiya had caught it while cutting palm fronds to trim as fans for her mistress and it had been yanked off. The penalty for taking off the collar was death and Kiya had little choice but to tie it together until she figured an alternative out. Nitetis had been too self-absorbed to notice her servant's collar was loose.

The collar came off streaked with blood. Even now Kiya hesitated before offering it. But what was the use in keeping it? She had no family, no mistress left alive. Her entire city was massacred. She had little hope of a future and the offering of the collar enforced this thricefold.

The collar rested awkwardly on the offering slab. It looked so small and inconsequential that Kiya sobbed as she realized she was lost. It was futile to ask for help when one had nothing to offer and even if she did, not all the gold in Egypt would tempt a god.

Kiya drew a deep, shaky breath, just as a pair of hands clamped over her mouth and she was forced back against a body that stank of blood and destruction. Sweat she was used to, but this smell was as vile as an animal's entrails lying in the sun.

The Roman soldier laughed as his hand roved down her body. "I got you. And you're primed for me. You knew I was coming." He ran a hand over her naked form, squeezing and kneading roughly. He spoke in her tongue to further humiliate her. "You are a fine woman by the feel of you." His hand painfully grabbed her breast and twisted the small nipple 'til Kiya cried out. He felt down and jabbed a filthy finger between her legs. "You're tight. I'm gonna be your first and your last. No need to even let the others have a go at you. Yeah, I like that. I'll be your only man in this life, pretty Egyptian bitch."

He looked around the temple, his eyes adjusting to the blackness. "What have we here? This flat rock is perfect for a fuck you'll never forget."

Just as he hoisted her onto the crude sacrificial altar, his companions crowded into the entry of the temple. "Sul, you got her? Why didn't you yell, you greedy bastard? I think I should fuck her first as your penalty and lack of fealty."

"Shut up, Gnaeus, and hold her arms. Cicero, get a hold of her leg."

Kiya's arms were grasped over her head and her leg clamped at the ankle, leaving her other to be forced wide by Sul. She heard the sound of clothing rustling; then felt something press against her, where she never thought she'd feel anything so awful. The burning was intense and something mashed against her opening.

"Damn it. I can't see and she's too tight."

A hand groped between her legs and pawed at her entrance, trying to hold her open and prone. Fingers jabbed and prodded. Kiya moaned and kicked as a fingernail scratched her sensitive passage.

Kiya's hands, still slick from blood, were held tightly, but Gnaeus lost his grip when she thrashed at the bumbling assault on her maidenhood. She reached down and clouted Sul solidly on the side of his head.

Sul howled with pain and reached up to grab her wrist, bending it cruelly. The clotting blood became a river as her wound reopened. Sul held her wrist and tried to force his cock inside her. She wriggled and began to scream.

"Turn her over and mash her face into the rock. I'm gonna do it to her so hard she screams for me to kill her. Then after you two are finished, we'll do just that." Sul spat a load of spittle from his mouth.

Kiya felt her arms twisted brutally, forcing her to roll over to lessen the pain. A resounding slap on her butt caused her to draw her knees under her. Her wrists were held down at her sides, her ass thrust up as Sul grabbed her ankles and pulled her legs out.

"Raise up, Egypt. You're about to get what's coming to you."

Kiya knew it was over. She could do nothing. The blood from her wrist ran freely, soaking the sacrificial slab and pooling in a sticky puddle under her body. Her face was pressed against the black rock, almost kissing it. Kiya felt tears run and mingle with the blood. She uttered one last plea, "Oh Great Taharqa, if you have any mercy, ease my suffering. I do not ask that my life be spared, only that I am allowed to die ignorant of the indignities being inflicted on me. Great One, hear my plea!"

Her ass was being clumsily pushed against and Kiya braced herself for the unknown assault. Then she wasn't sure what happened next. There was a rumbling and the sound of rocks falling. The temple shuddered and rocks tumbled from the ceiling in a mighty roar, as if the earth was being torn apart. The whole valley quaked and her attackers began to shout.

Fearful the entire valley was caving, and certainly the temple was collapsing, the soldiers dropped their holds on Kiya and scrambled for the entranceway. Two made it out, but one was knocked down by a falling rock.

Kiya lay on the altar, not sure what to do. The temple continued to rumble and the entranceway began to collapse. Black rock fell in a torrent as dust so thick it clogged the lungs, filled the air. Kiya knew she should try to escape as had the others, but her legs would not obey. She buried her head under her arms and waited for the end.

Kiya did not know how long she lay there. The darkness was now complete and no light above filtered into the temple. The settling dust tickled her nose and she could not help the delicate sneeze that erupted. The entrance of the temple was as dark as night and no airflow came from that direction. The temple entrance was buried, sealed with rock.

Kiya rolled over on the slab. She was not sure what to do. The temple was silent now except for the sound of a few rocks settling. As Kiya lay there she heard a moan from the Roman soldier, somewhere on the floor of the temple. She dared not move lest he not be as injured as she hoped, and attacked her again or just killed her outright.

Kiya's dark eyes darted around the temple. What was her fate? What was to become of her? Her blood had made the stone sticky and uncomfortable. She grew cold and shivered. In the darkness came an immense groaning from somewhere near the back of the temple, where it met the wall of the giant black pyramid. It sounded like a thousand laborers in pain, moving something heavy, followed by whispering such as no wind she had ever heard, uttered low and deep.

A whoosh sounded and scraping, like something being dragged across the stone floor. Then a light appeared from the back of the temple... No, a torch! Kiya stared, her eyes bulging. Was she hallucinating from the loss of blood? A figure appeared, then another. Dressed in gold plating and finely woven skirting these servants ignored Kiya and passed by the altar. Another moan came from the floor as the Roman soldier was hoisted and carried between the two men back through the temple and into the pyramid.

Kiya shivered and didn't know if she should indicate her presence. But what if she remained buried alive, starving and freezing? "Wait! What about me!"

From just inside the entrance to the pyramid, a deep chuckle rumbled. "Don't fret, pretty one. You belong to me."

"Who are you?" Kiya craned her neck, but she could see nothing. She struggled to rise, but her head swam. The voice seemed nearer, but she could discern nothing in the dark. He carried no torch and seemed to have no trouble finding his way towards her.

"I am the one you summoned. Your fresh blood cried out to me. Your tears became my tears. And so I have come for you."

From the darkness a large, black figure loomed. Kiya drew back, but the hands on her arms that helped raise her to a sitting position, were warm, and strangely soft with a furry texture.

The room careened dizzily and Kiya felt herself lifted into arms that were as warm as she was cold. The hard chest cradled her and she found herself crying in confusion, as her aching body sighed and fitted snuggly against her new captor. She was carried from the temple into the pyramid where no torches burned, but the figure carrying Kiya had no trouble seeing in the dark. He carried her for what seemed a lifetime down stone stairways and passages leading into eternity.

Kiya felt the softness of down and silk beneath her back. Kiya had lain on her mistress' pallet once when Nitetis was unaware, but this was far softer than any mere nobleman's pallet.

She sighed as her body relaxed and she felt the pain slowing moving through her. Was she dying? The voice in the darkness spoke low. "I can relieve your suffering. Would you like that? To feel no pain, to be free of earthly troubles and sorrows. Your city is gone; your life is no more. The man we have taken as an offering would have raped you and left you dead. I can keep you from that fate. Forever.

"I am revered, not just here, but all over the world. Wherever vengeance and retribution is sought is my realm. My kind must live on and for that to happen I must have a mate. I have chosen you. Your blood and tears called to me and lured me to the temple, but I cannot take you against your will, it is forbidden."

"I-I don't understand. What are you?" Kiya was more curious than scared to be face to face with a legend long whispered about. After what she had witnessed and faced that day, this seemed not scary, so much as bizarre.

"No. It is an unconditional contract. Binding by your agreement. My kind must flourish and to do that we must learn to adapt to the world above. And we must procreate in order that our children will live among the humans and guide them forward. Mankind is not the wisest species, but they are what has survived and changed the world, therefore we must blend with them."

Kiya did not know what that meant and latched onto her spiritual upbringing. "But you are Taharqa, fierce and known to exact revenge."

"I am Taharqa. In my own arrogance I thought I could strike a bargain with the gods and not pay a price. I achieved revenge on my brother and his wife. His lineage has perished. Now my penalty is to walk amongst the humans and wander the night. It is hard for a human to understand the loneliness, the solitude. But it must be so, until now."

"Now?" Kiya winced as her pained body contracted and muscles flexed.

Taharqa spoke low and persuasively. "Give me permission to ease your pain."

Another spasm racked Kiya's body as the blood loss cramped her muscles into waves of unrelenting torture. "Yes. Heal me. Please." She tried not to cry out.

A warm furred hand touched her brow, then ran down her cheek to her neck. An icy cold coursed wherever he touched, then warmth surged. Her shoulders practically melted into the soft bed on which she lay, leaving Kiya unprepared when he touched her bruised breasts. They tingled under his hands, unlike the fumbling touch of the Romans, and as they grew warm Kiya couldn't help but breathe, "More, please."

"Perhaps later, if…" Taharqa continued down her arm and stroked her wrist, leaving the statement unfinished.

The wound puckered and closed. Her fingers were rubbed and flexed. Her waist soothed 'til the bruises and scrapes disappeared. Her pubic region was scratched and tender as his touch lingered on her belly and his hand splayed down, erasing the marks as he went. He touched her delicate folds, his fingers moved within, so different from the earlier assault that Kiya felt tears gather.

He moved quickly, as if afraid to linger, and ran his furred hands high on her thighs, then down to her knees and calves. Her torn bloody feet were divested of their ragged slippers and rubbed 'til they were flawless.

"Turn over."

Kiya shuddered, remembering the soldiers.

"Trust me. I have saved you from a fate worse than death. I have asked permission to touch you. You have given it. If I was going to hurt you I would not have asked."

Kiya turned over, realizing the truth of his words. His touch on her buttocks was feather light as he smoothed her delicate skin, delving between the crack and her soft folds. Kiya was about to tell him he had already healed that part of her, but it felt so good to have him between her legs, she simply moved her legs further apart as he slipped his hand within.

She felt him push against her anus with his finger and wondered at the feel as he bent over her and kissed her plump cheek. "I would show you what it is to be completely taken, until you begged for it every night, but it would not be fair. You must come to me of your own free will."

His touch withdrew and she waited, but there was nothing. Light flooded the chamber as a torch was lit.

Puzzled, she turned around to find a huge black panther reclining next to her. Kiya shrieked in terror. These were the fabled big cats that could tear a man apart! As she scrambled to the front of the bed, the cat's shape became hazy and the outline shifted. The panther disappeared and in its place was an ebony-skinned man. Smooth of feature except for furry hands. His hair was lustrous black, his eyes such a bright emerald green they reflected light back at her. He stared at her intently. "Do I frighten you? Repulse you?"

Kiya ran her eyes over his body. Except for the fur on the back of his hands he looked like a man. But not like just any man. Taharqa was powerful even in repose. His thighs and arms were defined and the muscles flexed whenever he stretched.

With no shame he rolled onto his back. "I am neither man nor beast, but something in between." The fur on his hands disappeared.

"You change at will?" Kiya questioned, entranced.

"Yes. As it suits. Do I please you?"

Kiya ran her eyes down his chest, where no hair was now apparent. Only ebony skin, and more muscles. His stomach was flat and hard, smooth even down to where the lower abdomen met the beginning of pelvic bone. His cock and sacs were as black and smooth as the rest of him. As Kiya stared, his cock grew under her scrutiny. "You have no fur down there."

"I can have none, or some, or a lot. If you are mine, you may dictate whatever pleases you."

"I don't understand," Kiya questioned. "What does it mean to be yours?"

"Do you give me permission to show you?"

"Will it hurt?"

"I can make it pleasurable. But you must declare your vow to remain my mate. You cannot change your mind. The consequences are too great and my kind cannot venture amongst the humans freely just yet. Perhaps in a few more centuries when our children and grandchildren and so forth have evolved into a more blendable, accepted genus. Who can say? I only know I have been alone too long. Stay with me."

"Forever?"

"Forever," Taharqa answered truthfully.

"Show me pleasure and I will stay with you."

Taharqa smiled and his sharp white teeth vied with his glinting green eyes for brightness. He rolled onto his side, rubbing against Kiya as his fingers found her lips and parted them. His face came close and his lips pressed against hers. His tongue slid within and he slowly licked at her tongue. His hand found her breast and his thumb stroked the nipple back and forth, until it hardened and crested.

He ended the kiss and brought his head down until his mouth was at her breast. "I will suckle from you, just as our offspring will suckle from you and their offspring will nurse from their mothers for generations to come. We will grow strong through our offspring and populate the lands aboveground. Do you want this?" His tongue traced Kiya's areola until she arched her back excitedly.

"Yes. Oh, yes!" she gasped as his lips fastened on her nipple and sucked its tender bud almost ferociously.

His hand palmed her other breast, priming the nipple for his lips. He slid his body half over hers, allowing his hand to roam over her belly, relishing the slight rise of her abdomen. He couldn't wait to fill her with his seed that would result in his many offspring. His hand found her *mons* and cupped the crest. She was clipped of hair, as was their custom and he easily found the button that invited stroking.

Kiya rose up under his ministrations.

Taharqa pulled his head from her breast and watched her face as he slid a long finger into her cunt.

Kiya caught her breath in alarm. Would this hurt as when the soldiers had tried to rape her? Taharqa's cock was impossibly large. It would never fit! But his fingers were inside her, stroking, coaxing and Kiya was amazed when she felt a slide of liquid ooze from her womb.

"That's it, my sweet. Let your juices coat your passage to make way for me." His fingers moved within her until Kiya rode them in a rhythm that was designed to incite her to accept more of him. His fingers touched her deeply, his thumb stroking against her small pearlescent button in quick strokes. She rode his hand, but then it was gone.

Taharqa rose over her. "Touch me and guide me at your own pace."

Kiya's hand clutched for him almost spasmodically. She missed the feeling of him inside her. She wanted it back!

"Patience. That's it."

Kiya felt his swollen flesh against her hand, then in her palm. She closed over it, hearing Taharqa draw a ragged breath.

"You have no idea how long I've waited for you." Taharqa breathed as he pressed his cock against her entrance.

Kiya panicked. It was too big. It was going to be as with the soldiers!

She began to struggle under Taharqa and he pressed himself against her cunt, stroking her button with his cock, but not going further. "How does that feel? Good? Trust me. I can take you to paradise such as you have never dreamed. Feel this?"

He stroked her button until another slide of creamy juice formed at the entrance of her cunt. Then he pressed his cock against her and the tip slid inside. He continued to stroke against her. "Do you want more? Tell me what you want."

"More!" Kiya gasped, pleading for him not to stop. His cock slid deeper. She felt full as never before. The burning of her maidenhead was nothing compared to the sensation of his large cock lodged within her, pulling back then thrusting again. She rose against him, urging him to ride her faster, deeper.

Taharqa gauged her reactions and let his body move over hers accordingly. He had waited for this woman for centuries and now the time was here. He thrust into her to the hilt and was rewarded when Kiya locked her legs around him and bucked. He grabbed her ass and steadied her as he pumped against her, and with her, at the same time.

Kiya felt a wave coming, but did not know what would happen. The spiraling in her stomach traveled to her cunt then back up. Suddenly she was gripped with a sensation so powerful she screamed Taharqa's name, as he kept stroking her walls, finding her womb. Suddenly he stiffened above her, his muscles quivering as his balls released his seed and a hot spurt jettisoned deep inside

Kiya, causing her to clasp at Taharqa to capture all his essence.

They lay together, bodies twined as one. Taharqa voiced his thoughts. "You are satisfied? You will become my mate, the mother of my kind...our kind, the Felidaen."

Kiya laughed freely. "I am more than satisfied. I am yours. Forever."

Chapter One
Modern Day, U.S.

The small, plump, red tabby moved gracefully along the window ledge of the high-rise hotel stepping gingerly, alert but unconcerned. It might have been a mere ten feet off the ground, rather than a daunting twenty stories, for all the attention it paid to the danger. The pouch tied around the furry neck was no hindrance and the cat paid no heed as if accustomed to the added bulk. Over the side of the balcony and through the open sliding glass door the cat slipped silently, a small ghost in the darkness.

There was no hesitation in entering the hotel room and no confusion in the cat's actions, almost as if it knew the way and belonged there. But this cat called no man or woman its owner. The draw cord to the drape moved in the breeze and the cat batted at it playfully before moving on inside. The darkness held no challenge as the feline scanned its eyes around the room disdainfully, searching systematically every surface, every piece of furniture.

In mid-step the cat paused and cocked its head, listening. It raised its delicately sculptured head and sniffed the air, twitching its whiskers for extra sensation. There was the sweet smell of perfumed bath oil mingling with the humidity of a hot bath. A smell that was cloying yet unclean reached the cat, humans thought they were devoid of odor after bathing and scrubbing. Silly people, they reeked no matter what they did. Just as the bed sheets emitted the acrid scent of sex no matter how many times housekeeping washed the linen. There was always an underlying trace no matter what, and these bed sheets exuded an aroma that virtually screamed sex had taken place very recently.

The cat arched its back and leapt onto a chair, rubbing against it luxuriously. Humans with allergies were a favorite. When the room occupants came back from dinner and the man began sneezing, he would be clueless as to the cause. Sidetracked, he wouldn't think twice about noticing the missing items. Satisfied, the cat jumped down. Its four paws became hands and feet, its furred lithe body became a skin in human form, as naked it rose to two legs and walked to the dresser. Upon opening the top drawer, assorted socks and ragged boxer shorts were obvious, but nothing hidden underneath met the strange reflecting eyes. The other drawers were soundlessly opened and neatly searched, everything carefully returned to its place. The bedside table? Perhaps it held the sought-after prize.

The single drawer was crammed shut. It opened with a creak that made the form frown in the darkness. But no one stirred and unaccosted the she-line looked inside. The jumble sorted itself into a leather paddle, a large dildo and a smaller plug of some sort; an open box of glow-in-the-dark condoms, the individually wrapped packets strewn about the drawer for hasty groping and donning. The colors shrieked at the she-line's sensitive, dilated pupils and she growled deep in her throat. Humans were pigs! There was a leather mask and something else, a bulky packet underneath the mask. Ahh, what was this, hidden treasure? Inside the packet was cash. Hundred dollar bills, about ten grand. It would do, to start. Leaving a thousand dollars so at first glance it would fool a pair of weak-sighted human eyes, the she-line rolled the rest into a neat, tightfisted lump and placed it in the pouch around her neck. So much for foreplay, now where was the *pièce de résistance*?

Creeping on soft bare soles the lithe figure entered the compact bathroom. The smell of strawberry and hair products assailed her nostrils. How could humans breathe in this sauna-like atmosphere, not to mention copulate? For the smell of sex was in here as well. The medicine cabinet was empty and the cabinet under the sink held only extra towels. Her eyes darted to the towels piled next to the tub/shower combo. They were neatly folded except for the two that were lying discarded on the floor. All the towels were immaculately folded the same way except for the one on the bottom rack. It was backwards from the rest. Someone left-handed had folded this one. The she-line picked it up carefully and was rewarded with the sound of jingling. Unfolding the white soft cotton revealed what she sought. A garish diamond and sapphire necklace blazing with facets of reflected light even in the darkness. Ah, the sheer ugly beauty of it!

The necklace went into the pouch and the she-line smiled. Stealing from a thief was a reward in itself, especially when the thief was a two-bit swindler like Diamond Charlie. The she-line refolded the towel and replaced it. She went down on her knees and gathered herself for the transition. Her arms and hands became fur and paws and her body sinewy and agile. She mewed once and padded back out the balcony door and leaped onto the ledge. Once she was on the other side of the hotel the feline used the same room and balcony she had used to gain access to the ledge earlier that evening. The room was empty of occupants or belongings except for a pile of clothes on the floor. The tabby cat sat on the floor next to the clothes and transformed into a young woman with normal human features.

Tabitha Fenwick stretched her muscles in satisfied bliss before donning the black short skirt and emerald green turtleneck blouse that accentuated her almond-shaped eyes and yellow-green irises. The pouch she left tied around her neck over the blouse and under a black tailored Anne Klein jacket. Elegant yet understated, just the way Tabitha liked to appear. Her short, dark, auburn hair with its black streaks was sassy when she just combed her fingers through it, or sexy when she styled it in place. Right now it was the former and Tabitha couldn't have cared less. She slid her feet into a pair of kicky ruched black leather boots and stretched again just to get the kinks out.

She took the elevator up to the penthouse, using her security passkey to override the code to gain access to the top floors. The private domain of her boss, Brenton Calder, was out of bounds for many people, but not for Tabitha even in her human form. When the elevator opened, Tabitha smelled the overpowering cloying scent of perfume, expensive perfume, not the cheap knockoff but the real thing—Joy at two hundred fifty dollars an ounce. Brenton was occupied, it seemed. Tabitha used her passkey in the door and it opened readily enough. She walked stealthily into the vast room, careful her black high-heeled boots did not give her away. The lights were dim and the remnants of a candlelight dinner, replete with silver serving dishes, had yet to be cleared away.

Tabitha sniffed the air, *filet mignon*, not exactly her taste. She preferred fresh fish or roasted chicken. The dining area was devoid of humans. Likewise, the adjoining living room with the heavy dark furniture, gold gilt mirrors and picture frames hugging priceless masterpieces, was bare of life. A noise came from the bedroom. Ahh yes, Brenton *was* busy.

Tabitha laughed to herself. This mating thing the humans were always doing never ceased to intrigue her. She liked to watch and study the act, trying to analyze what made it so pleasurable. It looked nothing short of an awkward meeting of body parts, but still there must be something to make them repeat the act time and again. She sat on a padded ottoman and removed her boots before walking to the bedroom. It was dark, which was perfect for Tabitha. She could see without being seen, her elliptical pupils adjusting to the darkness quickly. There was a chair close to the bed that was adequate for her purpose. The bed itself was writhing with movement as forms took shape. There was Brenton lying on his back with some over-breasted blonde bent over his cock.

Tabitha watched as the blonde bobbed up and down on the phallus trying to take the whole of the shaft down her throat. Brenton was making a groaning noise deep in his own throat and his long tapered fingers were stroking the blonde's head, urging her on.

Tabitha sat back in the rattan fan-back chair and contemplated this new ritual. She knew the sex act was necessary to create life but why would one do it for any other reason? And certainly the blonde could not enjoy choking on Brenton's cock. She must find out more about this. The blonde made a gurgling noise in her throat as Brenton began to ejaculate. Tabitha judged by the sudden tensing of his muscles, he was climaxing. She wanted to taste what the blonde was tasting, feel the sensations she was feeling. Wasn't it said curiosity killed the cat?

Tabitha wiggled as warmth emanated from between her own thighs. She hoped she wasn't coming in heat. The tablets she took to keep her regulated and suppress the urge to mate had been working fine. Surely they were not failing her? Tabitha's fingers moved her skirt hemline higher. There was no faint odor of estrus so she was not in heat, but still there was a tingling between her legs as she watched the blonde release Brenton's now flaccid cock from her mouth. The blonde rose from the bed and unaware of her audience made her way unsteadily to the bathroom. Tabitha hoped she wouldn't hit the light switch before shutting the door, otherwise she might be spotted. She needn't have worried, as the blonde seemed disoriented and wobbled as she ran into the doorframe in the dark. Tabitha smothered a laugh. What a klutz!

The blonde took an eternity as the sound of the toilet flushing and the bathwater running came plainly to Tabitha's ears. She glanced to Brenton's sleeping form. He seemed unaware of the absence of his partner or of the noise in the bathroom. Tabitha tiptoed to the bed. Brenton's sandy-colored hair was disheveled against the pillow and his body was relaxed now that he had achieved release. She studied his broad chest, devoid of hair, and the nipples on his pecs that were puckered like tight little raisins. Tabitha reached inside her jacket and touched her own breasts through the turtleneck. Her nipples tightened as she traced a pattern around the areolas. Tabitha liked the feeling as she continued stroking herself while gazing at Brenton's tapered waist and the trail of hair leading down to his groin. Nestled in a patch of curly hair were his cock and balls. Apparently blondie hadn't done much other than suck him off, as his sacs were still full and rounded with unspilled seed.

Unable to help herself Tabitha's curiosity got the better of her and she knelt by the bed to get a closer look. His cock was still wet but it was impossible to tell if it was from the blonde's saliva or Brenton's jism.

However at the very tip was a bead of pearlescence that was hard to mistake. Tabitha carefully took a finger and blotted at the substance. She placed the drop on her tongue and considered it judiciously. It wasn't much but might have been a bit salty. She would have liked to lap up more of the milky white ooze the texture of thick cream, but there wasn't any left. Perhaps if she pulled on the two hanging sacs as one milked a cow's udder, she would be rewarded. And how hard did one have to pull? If she yanked too hard Brenton was bound to wake up. It was too dangerous.

Tabitha reached another tentative finger towards the cock. She traced the head as it lay innocuously nestled in repose just above the sacs. There was a stirring in the mushroom-like shape and she hastily moved her fingers away. They touched springy hair and warm flesh. Never having seen a man's organ so close Tabitha was powerless to leave it alone and like a magnet it drew her back. She batted at it playfully with her hand and it flopped gently back and forth. But then it stopped and stayed in place, looking thicker and stubbornly refusing to play her game.

Tabitha turned her attention to the sacs again. They were interesting, not quite round but like badly filled balloons, hanging dispiritedly. Tabitha rubbed one lightly with her thumb. The texture reminded her of peach skin, but the reddish-purple color left much to be desired. They weren't half as much fun as the cock in her opinion.

Returning to her favorite toy Tabitha ran her fingers along the base of the phallus, liking the velvety soft feel and the exciting pulsing beneath her fingertips. But then the entire shaft moved boldly, startling her overly alert senses.

Her reflexes were fast and she tried to jump back but a hand covered her own as Brenton's voice heavy with sleep and a faint rasp, came to her ears in the dark. "That's it, Meg." The hand over hers guided up and down the shaft as it expanded and flexed, like a hooded cobra rising to strike. "I want you tight around me, Meg. Come on, luv. Give me a ride before you go take your bath."

Tabitha gave a quick glance to the bathroom door. Apparently Meg was more interested in her bath than Brenton's good time. She couldn't very well just pull away and go running for the door and she did want to know about this mating for pleasure. On the other hand Brenton was her boss of only four months and Tabitha rather liked her job.

But it was about to get even more interesting. Tabitha wasn't worried about emotional entanglements. It wasn't her nature to become attached to humans and after she grew bored she would move on to another place of employment. Even if she did like watching Brenton, naked or clothed. He reminded her of herself. Graceful as a panther in his movements and sparing in his emotions. And she did like that lovely cock that she longed to play with for hours. It beat the hell out of a toy mouse.

But Brenton settled the matter for her. Meg apparently was not a closer when it came to sex and Brenton was used to taking matters in his own hand...literally. The hand covering Tabitha's loosened. Confused she drew back and watched as Brenton fisted his cock and pumped vigorously.

The bathwater was still running. Meg must be a soaker. Tabitha shrugged off her jacket but left her top on. The heavy pouch around her neck made her smile in double anticipation. She hiked her skirt above her waist and sat back in the wide rattan chair, splaying her legs apart.

She watched Brenton as he slowed his stroking, apparently savoring the feeling, in no rush to shoot his load. Tabitha reached between her own legs and fingered her clit lightly. It was damp and thickening as the blood pooled around it. Using her middle finger, it took little imagination to picture Brenton mounting her and probing at her cunt entrance.

Tabitha had watched enough of this sex between couples to know where things went and as her hand rested against the inside of her thigh she projected it was Brenton's silken touch as his aroused shaft probed insistently. She reached between her legs and guided him to her. She had all the right parts for this experiment and was human enough to feel a rush of her own wetness against his straining member as the broad head nudged her vaginal lips open. She basked in the feeling of him probing within but she was tight and his progress was halted.

Impatiently Tabitha let out a frustrated mewl that went unheeded in the darkness. But nature took over and a thick slide of lubrication discharged from her womb and aided in assuring the cock would gain admittance. Tabitha couldn't help the moan as he eased into her.

She pushed two fingers deep inside herself trying to absorb all the sensations at once. No, they weren't her fingers. It was Brenton's cock that made her tingle, burn, shiver and want to purr all at the same time. There was slight pain at first but that itself was an added nuance to the experience.

Brenton muttered in the velvety darkness, further adding to the fantasy. He moved his hips in rhythm to his hand stroking his cock, back and forth, slow and deliberate. It was easy to imagine the fingers Tabitha rotated inside herself were that thick pulsing cock, a glorious animal in its own right as it skimmed over textured walls that gripped it one moment then kissed it with dew the next.

Tabitha fantasized the friction and rhythm of Brenton's rolling hips and his velvety cock as it bored within her and caused her to instinctively ride the motion. She would love to feel Brenton's lips on her breasts, licking them and sucking them into hard peaks that were nothing like the usurped Meg's pendulous orbs, but were finely molded and made for a man's lips. Brenton's lips.

Tabitha gasped as a delicious ripple radiated from her cunt. She watched Brenton's face, trying to preordain when he would peak so she could time hers to match. Even in her heightened sexual state she mused how handsome Brenton was despite the intense emotional strain of pre-orgasm.

But damn, this experiment into human sexuality would have to end quickly. Already the taps in the bathroom were turned off and the sound of a towel being jerked off the rack met her sensitive ears. Tabitha tried to recapture her fantasy. She rode Brenton hard, feeling him bulging within her, straining to achieve release. Her fingers were soaked with her own juices as they worked frenetically imitating the cock she so craved to feel inside her.

Brenton jerked as he began to come. Tabitha imagined reaching for his sacs and stroking them as with a gust of air Brenton exhaled and shot his load. A curious jet of thick liquid that should have shot deep up inside Tabitha pooled on Brenton's belly and made Tabitha squirm as she gasped and twitched with an orgasm that left her breathless.

She watched Brenton as she tried to stand but her legs wobbled. She sank back on the chair focusing on Brenton's face in the darkness, replete with satisfaction as his fickle cock nestled back down against his thigh. His sleepy deep voice in the darkness startled her into action. "Meg, bring me a towel, would you?"

The sound of the bathroom door being pulled open brought Tabitha to her feet. She grabbed her jacket and was out the bedroom door in a flash. The wetness between her legs cooled as she ran, leaving her still tingling as contractions in her cunt signaled she had been too hasty and her body wanted more. More Brenton…about eight inches more.

Tabitha wanted time to ponder this new experience she'd heard was called lust, but there wasn't even seconds to spare. She grabbed her boots in the living room and was outside the suite before she slowed to a normal speed. She would come back in the morning and see Brenton. Tonight he would sleep in blissful ignorance thinking it was Meg who had been enjoying his performance.

Tabitha returned to her own room two floors below the penthouse and shucked off her jacket. The pouch around her neck drew her immediately but her session with Brenton had left her sweaty and sticky, and her finicky habit of cleanliness demanded she bathe and wash. She threw the pouch on the bed then went directly to the shower. She hated water. Really hated it. But it was a necessity to good grooming. The antibacterial soap she used was mild but to her sensitive nostrils it still smelled clinical. She washed between her legs, wishing it had truly been Brenton's cock lodged inside her, moving and sliding, triggering small sensations that radiated through her body until she kneaded her nails like claws, in ecstasy. That beautiful cock! Somehow she had to have another session with the silken toy she so craved further knowledge of.

Yes, she had to have it inside her for real! She would, she vowed as she remembered how it had stood erect waiting for her touch, waiting for her cunt to slide over it and fit it deep inside. If only she could make it happen. Tabitha's hand touched her clit and she shivered. Her body still hungered for Brenton.

She massaged herself back and forth until her legs trembled, her hand moving quickly, bringing her to a low cry of unsatisfied release. Again she pushed two fingers deep inside her cunt, imagining Brenton doing this to her, replacing fingers with that wonderful phallus that spouted a creamy potion like fine liqueur. She could almost feel him sliding in and out, pulsing within her. Tabitha pressed hard against her hand, rubbing the nub that fed her release. She quaked to orgasm just as she had before, but this time she promised, her fingers would soon be replaced by Brenton's cock and he was going to be wide-awake when it happened.

She toweled off, then transformed, making sure her coat was groomed silky smooth by her sandpaper tongue. Then satisfied she was clean. Tabitha leaped onto the bed, transforming in mid-jump. She landed naked on her knees next to the pouch. The diamond and sapphire necklace she left inside. The nine thousand in cash she stuffed between the mattresses. Then with a purr she curled up on the bed in a pose similar to a fetal position, and fell asleep.

Chapter Two

Tabitha was up and around early as was her habit. She ordered from room service a delectable Alaskan smoked salmon omelet, coffee with real cream, left the coffee untouched and drank the cream before making her rounds. Officially her shift as security officer of the Arpel hotel did not begin until 8 a.m. but she liked to prowl around the building earlier. Because she neither looked nor dressed the part, she was far more effectual than a uniformed security officer. Although Brenton had hem-hawed about hiring her because of her small stature, that soon changed as Tabitha had demonstrated her quick reflexes and ability to disable an opponent with her knowledge of nerve touch.

She'd winced when Brenton had called her a Trekie fan at her initial interview and he'd given her the corny Star Trek Vee signal with his fingers. Tabitha had resisted giving Brenton a finger all right. She suspected he was baiting her as she was very serious about her job and Brenton, being the self-made millionaire and pain in the ass owner of the hotel, liked to test his employees' stress level concerning customer service. So Tabitha had merely smiled politely at Brenton's weak humor and had gotten the job.

Brenton might be a pain in the rear smart aleck but he did allow for idiosyncrasies, which boded well for Tabitha. Tabitha worked until 7 p.m. with two hours off around noon. Brenton never asked why she needed the two hours off and Tabitha was glad because she was not about to admit she took a catnap in the afternoon and preferred late hours. She very much doubted Brenton would understand it was her inherent nature. Not to mention Tabitha was the runt of a large litter and all of her close family had tails and purred when content. No better just to pretend she was an eccentric normal person and needed two hours downtime during the day.

At eight Tabitha caught the elevator up to the penthouse. Davey, the elevator operator, who was approaching sixty and still liked to be called Davey and not the mature Dave, smiled at her. "You look very pretty, Miss Tabitha."

Tabitha tried to play nice and smile but she was ambivalent about the compliment. Sure, she had meant to look particularly attractive when she'd chosen the beige and black wrap dress that accentuated her figure for her interview with Brenton. The mirrored back wall of the elevator proved one of the two things Tabitha knew about Brenton; he loved his expensive clothes and his tall blonde women. And Tabitha could not afford the first except at outlet prices and she sure as hell was never going to be the second. She sighed. Worse, she suspected Brenton was a dog person.

Tabitha resisted pacing the elevator. For one thing her croc-textured black sling-back pumps made a whoosh noise when she walked, that was as embarrassing as it was irritating. And for another, Davey would never understand her anxious reaction to closed spaces. He might think her claustrophobic but if she got in a dither and her breathing accelerated rapidly, she might transform and there was no way in hell Davey was going to mistake her paws for opposable thumbs.

It was a reoccurring nightmare Tabitha had to be caught in a stuck elevator with no way out. By the time she was rescued her fur was more than just ruffled; she was stuck in mid-transformation, neither woman nor beast. So far transformation had always been complete and as far as was known it was just an urban legend among her genus that it could happen, but urban legends were known to have their roots grounded in reality!

But they reached the penthouse without incident and Davey winked at her before the elevator door closed on his grandfatherly countenance. Tabitha knocked once then slid her passkey in the slot. If Brenton was indecent he'd had a warning. But when Tabitha entered it was to find Brenton sitting at the ornately carved Louis XV dining table reading the morning paper and sipping orange juice while eating a blueberry muffin. Alone. Apparently blondie was a half-nighter and hadn't stayed for breakfast.

Tabitha sniffed the air. The perfume odor was stale; yep, blondie was gone. And Brenton was alone and dressed, well sort of. He wore freshly creased slacks of gray wool and cashmere but no shirt. Tabitha tried not to stare too hard at the nipples she had studied the night before. How dense could a man be not to be able to tell a woman was giving him the once-over at the breakfast table?

Tabitha admired the way Brenton's chest tapered down at the waist and his flat stomach beckoned her to slide her tongue over the hard surface and trace the path from his belly button down the sprinkle of light colored hair that ran inside the top of his pants. She wanted to devour his cock much as he was devouring that blueberry muffin. The mushroom head was made for sucking and she could curl her tongue around the shaft and milk him until he shouted for mercy.

Tabitha fantasized Brenton's muffin-filled hand was palming her breast, raising it until the areola was upturned to his lips where he slowly pressed it to his mouth, taking in just the tip and sliding his tongue over the tiny sensitive creases until it hardened. Then he ran his tongue over and around the soft, satiny skin, taking the nipple within and suckling it while his other hand moved between her legs and sought her cunt. God, she wished there'd been more time last night! A noise startled Tabitha from her sexual reverie.

Brenton had spoken and Tabitha realized she had not heard a word. "I'm sorry?"

"I said I'd wished there'd been more time."

"What?" *Was he a mind reader?*

"To retrieve the necklace. I know it was short notice to tell you yesterday afternoon and expect you to just waltz in and retrieve it."

Tabitha smiled at her thoughts. He didn't know. Of course not. "It was no problem."

"Then you have it?"

Tabitha reached under the neckline of the wraparound dress and pulled at the strap that held the pouch around her neck. She threw the velvet bag at Brenton.

He caught it deftly with one hand, the other still clutching the corner of the newspaper. Taking his time he wiped his mouth on a napkin then opened the pouch and shook out the diamond and sapphire necklace. "Ugh! It's ghastly!"

"Yes. But worth a great deal," Tabitha reasoned.

"But something of value should also be beautiful to look at."

"Beauty is…"

"Yeah. Yeah. In the eye of the beholder," Brenton finished.

"I was going to say, 'Beauty is overrated'."

"Whatever."

Brenton was clueless what she meant. Not surprising. If he didn't know Tabitha wanted him, he sure wasn't going to acknowledge she was far more suited for him than the jism-choking blonde. Humans! They practically had to have the truth shoved up their asses before they realized it! Tabitha was as frustrated as if she was chasing her tail and that she rarely did.

"How did you get it away from that skank Diamond Charlie?"

Tabitha smiled. "I waltzed in and retrieved it."

Brenton would naturally assume she'd used her security pass card and walked into Diamond Charlie's room. And indeed, Tabitha could have done just that, but why add the risk of being seen by someone entering the room? Her way was far more effective and foolproof.

"I can skip into Agatha Winters' suite and return it just as easily," she assured Brenton.

"No. I can't let you do that." Brenton was staring at Tabitha like a cat that was stalking a goldfish. If he didn't wipe that devil-may-care bedroom smile off his face, Tabitha swore she would cream her panties right there and then.

Brenton seemed to have lost his train of thought. It wasn't like him and Tabitha wondered what was on his mind. She glanced at him and caught him eyeing her legs. Tabitha caught her breath. Was he interested in her? A girl could dream.

But he seemed to be back on track. "Uh, Agatha Winters had security cameras installed in her suite yesterday. No, it's better I return the necklace to her on the up and up."

"You can't very well tell her your security was lacking the night of the charity ball when Diamond Charlie snatched it from around her neck, with no one the wiser, until she discovered it was missing when she looked at herself in the ladies' room mirror."

"Yeah, that's the last time I hire a private security firm and give mine the night off. You'd think if you hire professionals you get better quality than the help you hire off the street."

"Hey! You hired me off the street! You told me to go away for the night remember? You said the ball was too important to trust with minor hotel security. You said—"

"Shut up! Like I need the reminder. Anyway, the necklace is back and I'll tell Agatha it was found in the laundry chute."

"Like she'll believe that! Are you going to convince her it was lost in her brassiere?" Tabitha scoffed, Brenton was rankling her fur.

"I don't have to be specific. She can draw her own conclusions how it got there. Perhaps it fell off before the ball and got mixed up with the linen or towels. Hell, she'll be so glad to see it, it won't matter how."

"Just smile and look pretty when you tell her and she'll believe anything." Tabitha watched Brenton's facial expression.

He looked annoyed. Agatha Winters was well into her sixties and known to be on the prowl for another husband. Number four to be exact and Brenton was on her list of prospects. She liked her men young and studly. At thirty Brenton filled the bill, not to mention he could circulate in her upper echelon circles without social training.

"Don't you have a job to do?" Brenton tried to change the topic.

"Sure. Uh, how was your night last night? I mean, while I was waltzing into thieves' hotel rooms."

"Nothing special. I had dinner with a friend and early bed. I have to stop eating beef before bedtime though. It gives me the most peculiar dreams."

Tabitha wondered what he would say if she confessed it hadn't been a dream and she had been in his room masturbating with him, and imagining she was riding his hard delicious cock until he exploded inside her. Would he let her explore his body and discover what made men and women crave sex so much? She wanted to take her sandpaper-rough tongue and run it over his cock until it stood at attention. She wanted to lick his balls until they ached and she wanted to taste more of his jism, lapping his cum like the cream she had lapped up that morning for breakfast. She would make him see she was special, indeed! In more ways than one. But of course she said nothing, did nothing, and only smiled mysteriously.

Brenton seemed to watch her in contemplation. Tabitha wondered if he ever looked at her breasts the way his eyes caressed his buxom dates and bed companions. Did he see anything attractive in his newest security officer? Damn! Why was she even thinking about that, this morning? It wasn't like Tabitha to dwell on human feelings. And this morning she was in sexual overdrive.

She had better check the calendar. Perhaps it was the time of the month to double up on her hormones and decrease her omega intake. She could not risk coming in heat and having to isolate herself when she was so new to the job. How would she explain that to her boss? *Uh, Brenton... I know I've only been here four months, but I need seven to ten days off or I'll strip and drop to my knees and beg you to penetrate me from behind and fuck me continuously for a week while I yowl and claw at you.* Yeah, that would go over real well and what kind of referral would it get her?

"Is something funny?" Brenton asked. "Care to share why you have that smirk on your face?"

"No. What do you suppose Diamond Charlie will do when he discovers the necklace is gone?"

"What can he do? No, he'll chalk it up to a thief robbing a thief and cut his losses. Good work, Tabitha. Now that your three-month probationary period is up, we should get together and discuss what would keep you satisfied here at the Arpel. I don't want to lose you to competition. Is there anything I can do to ensure your loyalty and fealty?"

Yeah, unzip your pants and let me lick and suck you until you're rock-hard, then do to me what I dream of doing to you. But Tabitha kept her wayward thoughts to herself and tried to beam a grateful employee smile at her boss. "I'm just happy to do my job. It's not often a boss lets his employees call him by his first name."

"It's my philosophy to trust my employees and treat them like extended family."

"You are a prince among men." *And a Tom among cats.*

"Tabitha. You are so maddening when you fire retorts back at me. I can't tell if you're serious or having a joke at my expense. Sometimes I just want to…" He was on his feet and Tabitha thought she must be dreaming again as he pulled her roughly against him and pressed his lips against hers, raising her off the ground to his height. She was pinned to his bare chest and her own breasts hardened instantly. She growled deep in her throat and tangled her arms around his neck.

His hands were low on her back, pressing her to him. She swore the bulge in his pants was growing larger. She could not help rubbing against him to indicate her need. It was instinctual and felt so right.

His tongue slid inside her mouth and ran along her teeth then settled deep within. He pressed her even tighter until Tabitha made a mewling noise that signaled she needed air. That's all she wanted. That and Brenton to make love to her until they both fell into an exhausted stupor.

But the slight noise seemed to bring Brenton to his senses and he stepped back, quickly. "This isn't right."

"What!" Tabitha almost yelled. "It's perfect!"

"It's impossible."

"Because you're my boss? I quit! Problem solved." Tabitha saw a shadowed frown on Brenton's face, she did not understand.

Nonetheless he smiled slightly at Tabitha's quick retort. "It's not that simple, Tabitha. It's impossible for reasons I can't explain."

"It's because I'm not beautiful like those other girls you date, isn't it? You don't want to cramp your reputation with the likes of me, is that it?"

"That's not…" But Brenton changed his mind and instead almost painfully rasped out. "Yeah, that's it."

Tabitha stared hard then to her horror tears gathered and threatened to spill down her face. There was no way in hell she was going to let that man see her cry! No way! She turned her back and slammed from the suite without looking behind.

* * * * *

Tabitha purposefully stayed away from Brenton for the next few days and concentrated on her job. Agatha Winters did not raise a peep at the return of her diamond and sapphire necklace and neither did Diamond Charlie at his loss of it. Charlie checked out of the hotel and Tabitha figured that was that.

A few nights later Tabitha the she-line, unable to sleep, was prowling on the hotel ledge high above the street when she heard the unmistakable sounds of whimpering and begging coming through a balcony door. It was her job to check it out and if it was something that would cause a blight on the hotel, Tabitha could always go around and transform to human form and knock on the door as hotel security checking out a noise complaint. She was on the tenth floor and the rooms here were comfortable, but not the most exclusive, so it could be any guest doing heaven only knew what to a wife or girlfriend.

Nimbly Tabitha jumped onto the balcony and slinked through the door, ducking behind a chair as the room was lit and she didn't want to be seen. Peering carefully from around the chair, a strange sight met her feline eyes.

A man was lying tied to one of the double beds, with neckties binding his wrists to the wooden bed frame. He was clothed in a ladies' pink sheer negligee with nothing underneath. He was morbidly obese; the rolls of flesh around his middle almost obscuring his meager organ and sacs. As Tabitha watched, a woman clad in a red leather outfit with a spiked collar and thigh-high patent leather red boots walked up and down the floor between the beds and yelled obscenities at the man. She carried a flogger and occasionally dealt the man a smack, miraculously close to his groin but missing his penis by mere inches. She continued to yell and flog until the flaccid penis began to perk up. Stubbornly it remained at half-mast.

The woman had a mass of red hair coiled around her head like a beehive and bright garish red lipstick. She wore heavy makeup, punctuated by vivid peacock blue eyeshadow and false eyelashes. She began to jump up and down in a tantrum and Tabitha almost transformed out of shock when she saw the woman had an Adam's apple that bobbed up and down when she jumped. What was this strange she-man?

The she-man began to shriek; "I knew it! I knew it! I don't excite you anymore, you whore! Our weekend away is ruined because you can't get it up for me! No one is limp for Stevie, no one! Do you hear me!" The she-man jumped on the bed and stood over the prostrate form. The red leather outfit was split at the crotch and the she-man's testicles were clearly visible. The flogger was brandished for effect and whistled through the air. The she-man named Stevie brought it down on his own scrotum. He shrieked. "You see what you've brought me to? You see what your Stevie has fallen to?"

For the first time the man on the bed spoke. "My love, untie me. Let me hold you."

The she-man flogged himself again, crying sharply, "I dare not! You do not truly love me."

"I do. Look! My cock rises for you and only you!"

Tabitha looked and sure enough the half-mast penis was at full attention, puny though it was. The one called Stevie shrieked with glee and fell to his knees, hastily untying the man in the pink negligee and turning about-face, in a prone position. Without preamble the pink negligee fluttered to life as the fat man threw himself at Stevie and rammed his cock through the split in the red leather. Stevie uttered a guttural high-pitched cry then called out expletives as his paramour rode him.

Tabitha had never seen this mating habit before. Men who were womanish and women who were men! It was all so confusing. And how did it feel to have a cock rammed into your anus? For some reason she thought of Brenton and his large member, swollen and glistening, plunging in and out of her rear. Intriguing. A contraction in her cunt and her ass simultaneously took her by surprise. She would leave the she-men to their games and contemplate this new feeling and what she had seen. And how could she get Brenton to do this to her?

Chapter Three

Tabitha had the next day off for personal reasons. Her three-month doctor's appointment was routine. The shot of Depo-Provera was a godsend for three months protection of birth control. If Tabitha did happen to have breakthrough estrous she certainly did not want what had happened to her sister Felicia to happen to her.

Felicia was a beautiful tortoiseshell Persian who had gone slumming one night in the alleys of the city. The result was Tabitha's nephew Leo, who had to be home-schooled until he achieved transforming control. Mind over matter was no principle for a rambunctious child to learn easily. Not that Leo wasn't a great kid, but Tabitha wasn't ready for that kind of responsibility. There was also a high chance of multiple births and that was one experience Tabitha could live without. She had seen what her mother had gone through with a litter of five that had led to stringent rules for her and her siblings. Trying to enforce those rules on a subspecies that was prone to roam at night and stay away for days at a time was no picnic.

After Felicia's debacle the rules had been tightened to the extreme. Tabitha's freedom had been curtailed to the point she could never go out alone or unescorted by a chaperone. In by dark and no transforming outside the house. And so Tabitha had reached adulthood on the naïve side where sex was concerned. She was brought up understanding birth control was a necessity and estrus should be cautiously allowed for health reasons but only under controlled conditions, i.e., when safe and isolation possible. If it hadn't been for her rascal of a brother Tom, Tabitha might have remained naïve.

Tom was a bad boy and considered Trouble Deluxe, though his sleek good looks and carefree attitude let him get away with almost anything. In this case Tabitha had found her brother's stash of adult magazines tucked between his mattresses, when she had been wandering through his room. Well, Tabitha had actually been snooping. Her brother was a mystery to her. She adored him and his carefree spirit, coming and going through the window in the dead of night, ignoring the house rules.

The magazines were only the tip of the iceberg. In his closet, tucked under a stack of old comic books were videos. At first Tabitha hadn't been sure why Tom had a copy of Alice in Wanderlust and Debbie Does Dallas, Part 1 and 2. Who was this Debbie and what was she doing in Dallas?

The answer was soon apparent as Tabitha snuck the tapes into the living room, late at night and stuck one in the VCR. By the time Debbie finished with Dallas, Tabitha was equally informed. Everything would have been fine if her mother hadn't woken up and her alert ears picked up the sound of moaning and groaning coming from the living room.

Was one of her kittens hurt? She tried to watch them like a hawk, but they prowled so, it was difficult to watch them 24/7. She only hoped one hadn't darted in front of a car. She scrambled out of bed and padded downstairs.

There in the living room, Tabitha sat in front of the large screen TV, her eyes huge, watching porn. Mrs. Fenwick let out a yowl that would have awakened the entire household, had anyone been home. Not only was it discovered her daughter was watching X-rated movies, but all of her other children were absent, having snuck out. Thank God Seline was at her grandmother's. Felicia and Tommy were the errant ones.

Mrs. Fenwick shook her head in disappointment at her middle daughter. Certainly Tabitha had lacked the skills necessary to be helpful to her grandmother, but this-this went beyond clumsiness and inattentive behavior.

The movies were confiscated and Tabitha placed on restriction and Tom...well, Mrs. Fenwick could not help the soft spot in her heart for her only son. He was a charming rogue and she couldn't stay mad at him for long.

But even a spanking could not dispel the images Tabitha had seen on the screen, close-up, in vivid color. Wow. Curiosity may have killed the cat, but what a way to go! Tabitha vowed, someday she would find someone special to try out those engrossing positions and wildly uninhibited actions on. It couldn't be just any ol' randy human with alley cat tendencies. It had to be someone special, someone irresistible and alluring. Now Tabitha had found that person and she knew it was Brenton Calder.

The more she thought about it, the more determined she became. And Tabitha knew just the person who could help her achieve her single-minded goal.

* * * * *

After her doctor's appointment Tabitha drove her midnight blue Mazda Miata over to the older part of the city where elegant and stately large homes in Victorian architecture perched on the hillside overlooking the valley. As she wound her way up the narrow drive towards a hulking residence, the bushes and dense old growth of hedges and magnolia trees rustled with sparrows and robins. Tabitha's acute hearing could pick out every nuance of twittering and wings fluttering. She tried to keep her attention span on the road but it was so hard not to dart her head this way and that, eagerly watching the nervous birds. Maybe she'd have time to do a little hunting after she had fulfilled her mission and spent some time with her grandmother.

Tabitha's grandmother from her mother's side of the family was descended from a long line of witches' familiars. Grandmother's knowledge of herbs and remedies and such was uncanny. Tabitha always felt guilty when she visited the old residence on the hill and she tried to be especially attentive to her grandmother whenever she talked about her craft.

The fact was Tabitha had been slated to be apprenticed to her grandmother and learn all the secrets and lore that would be passed on for more generations than could be counted. But that was the problem, Tabitha was number deficient. She measured potions in error. A dash of this, a pinch of that. Or was it a half cup or quarter teaspoon? She must also learn Spellspeak, a mixture of Latin, Gaelic and Bodiccean. But Tabitha's attention span was nil and after several near tragic consequences and mis-spells that resulted in one unscheduled eclipse and a thirty second time lapse in the western time zone, she was expelled and her sister Seline was apprenticed in her place.

Dear, sweet Seline, who was thought too gentle to be a proper familiar, was the last hope for a direct female descendant. Though she had a green eye and a blue eye, which was not considered a desirable trait in a familiar, she was sleek and black, and attentive which overrode her shortcomings. The deciding factor was Seline's penchant for numbers, and her spells were mixed with exactness and precision care. This was something Tabitha would never achieve despite years of tutoring.

Seline greeted Tabitha from the sunny padded seat in the large bay window at the front of the house where she was drowsing in the sun. Her dual-colored eyes glittered in recognition and she stretched her furry form languidly before leaping down behind the heavy velvet curtains and appearing in human form at the door, a terrycloth robe hastily wrapped about her dark form.

Tabitha was just climbing the steps to the wide porch as Seline beckoned her in. "Come in! Tabitha, you look terrific. Like the cat that swallowed the canary! You didn't, did you?" Seline's long dark hair swirled around her, as she looked worried. Seline was too gentle to hunt birds or mice and she hated the thought of her siblings being less considerate.

Tabitha laughed. "No, I like my meat cooked or at least steamed, except fish. Thank heavens for sushi!" So much for her having a chance to hunt, Tabitha sighed. Seline would have a fit if Tabitha caught so much as a mouthful of feathers. Sisters were such pains! She wondered if her grandmother still kept a well-stocked koi pond. "Is Grandmother around?"

"Of course but she's sleeping. She had a late night last night, it being a full moon and all."

"I'd forgotten her responsibilities. Did you go with her?"

"No. Gram says I'm not ready to be indoctrinated into the coven yet. But soon!"

"Well, I'll just visit with you until she wakes up then. I hope she has the potion I need."

"Ooh, I have been well-schooled in mixing potions." Seline tried not to brag. "Remember when Gram had you mix gotu-kola with catnip and you got high on the catnip and started chasing your tail until you got too dizzy? I'll never forget finding you lying in the kitchen floor, muttering about *'gotta koala, gotta koala'*." Seline giggled.

"Don't rub it in, sis. I'm the first to admit I'm not cut out for the higher learning of Spellspeak. But this potion is in Grandmother's locked cabinet."

Seline's eyes grew wide. "Oh, it's one of the forbidden ones."

"Yeah well, something has come up that I need to know."

"Need to know? Or are curious?" Seline laughed.

"Same thing when you're a cat," Tabitha shot back.

"But Tabitha those potions are dangerous and unpredictable," Seline cautioned. "That's why only Gram administers them."

"I know. That's one of the few things that stuck in my mind through my apprenticeship debacle. But Grandmother said if ever comes a time when the problem outweighs the side effects to come to her. So here I am."

"Sounds very serious."

"If I'm going to survive in this human world, I have to understand certain things."

Seline gasped, "You're talking about S-E-X!" She spelled out the letters in a whisper.

Poor Seline, she was even more in the dark about mating habits than Tabitha. But for Seline it would have to stay that way until she reached thirty or her power would be drastically diminished. Tabitha was forbidden to even broach the subject with her sister. "You know I can't say any more, Seline. I'll wait for Grandmother."

"Okay. You want to chase each other around the house?"

The sisters never outgrew a game of tag. Once inside and the door firmly shut, the two transformed and took off at a dead run through the halls and under chairs, jumping onto the piano and racing across the ivory keys, causing them to crash notes in discord. Tabitha jumped onto the coffee table in the living room and, too late caught sight of the vase of roses in the middle. The table had been recently polished and her paws slid without traction. She sideswiped the vase, causing it to tip over. Roses, water and Tabitha ended up on the hardwood floor. Tabitha transformed and lay naked in a puddle of water cursing under her breath.

Seline peeped around the corner of the hall, cautiously, before transforming and rising to two legs, finding her robe and making herself decent.

"That vase was not there the last time I was here!" Tabitha accused.

"Sorry." Seline hid a giggle. "You look like a drowned cat!"

"It's not funny, Miss Goody Two Paws!" Tabitha splashed the water in Seline's direction.

Seline jumped back. "Stop it or I'll tell!" Her voice rose two octaves as her fear of water took over.

"'Fraidy cat!" Tabitha taunted loudly.

A voice from the stairway carried down. "What is all that racket down there? Seline, is someone here?"

Instantly Seline straightened up and called back in a grown-up lilt. "It's Tabitha, Gram. She needs to see you."

The voice came again, this time in a growlish tone. "For heaven's sake, why didn't you wake me? You'd think I was ancient the way you coddle me, Seline. I am fourteen in cat years, only seventy in human. I fancy I have a few lives." The sound of slow shuffling footsteps on the stairs changed to the pitter-patter of soft paws. A pudgy, blue-gray, medium-haired feline appeared at the foot of the impressive carved staircase. Back on even ground, the gray changed into an older woman. Both girls politely glanced away from the naked form until the gray wrapped herself in a bright flowery housecoat kept handily on a coat rack next to the newel post.

The older woman breathed a sigh, "It's so much easier to negotiate the stairs on four legs instead of two. Redistribution of body weight is the only way to go on inclines and declines." She paused at the sight of her naked granddaughter lying on the floor. "Now what have you gone and done? My vase! My flowers!"

"Sorry, Grandmother. We were playing and —"

"Playing? At your age? And where are your clothes? You are too old to be cavorting about like kittens," she admonished as Seline found the pile of Tabitha's jeans and lacy top and held them out to her sister.

Seline was engrossed in Tabitha's thong underwear. "What are these?" The stretchy piece of fabric dangled from her fingers.

"They're my delicates!" Tabitha tried to be diplomatic. She knew how hard it was on Seline to stay celibate and the poor girl had six more years to go.

"They sure don't look like my underwear!" Seline quipped.

"Nor mine." Grandmother looked disapproving.

Tabitha grabbed the tiny bit of material and turned around to don them. She hastily shimmied into her jeans. "I saw them in a catalog. The humans wear them, it seems they like the way they fit."

"Well, it looks darned uncomfortable to have a string between your nether regions if you ask me. You shouldn't take up all those human customs," her grandmother warned.

Tabitha fought with her bra to get the straps straight. How was she going to broach the subject with her grandmother about her reason for coming? But Seline knew she was forbidden certain topics and made a simple excuse. "I'll clean this up and get more water in the vase."

She was gone as Tabitha finished dressing and was tying her shoelaces. "Grandmother, I have been observing the humans and their mating habits. I have questions that cannot be answered and must be felt. I am cautious and take precautions and I want to be equally careful with whom I mate. But the one I have chosen does not choose me."

Her grandmother looked at her from shrewd green eyes. "You cannot force someone to touch you. It is forbidden."

"I know the rules. He must willingly come to me. But do the rules not state if he has willingly given himself once, then does not desire me any longer, I may seek aid?"

"You have been intimate with this human?"

Technically it was true. Well, sort of in Tabitha's mind, so she nodded. "Yes."

"And now he does not want to honor the bargain, accept his responsibility?"

Tabitha fought against showing her unease at twisting the rules of the revered Spellspeak. "He kissed me and we experienced sexual release together but now does not desire me."

Her grandmother shook her head. "You have chosen wrong, but you made the choice. He must honor your choice. It is written that once a Felidaen with his or her body has honored any human, if the Felidaen so desires, the union can be enforced. Do you swear on ancient honor that he wished it as much as you?"

"Oh, yes. He wished it very much at the time. I still wish it; he does not. I have tried to overcome the thoughts and feelings that have come over me at odd times but I cannot."

"It is often such when you have bonded. Our kind is aloof and distant but once we attach ourselves to a human, it is strong and lasting. Even if the human does not feel the same way. But that can be remedied. So be it. Come with me."

The older woman led the way to the kitchen. They passed Seline on her way back with the vase of water and roses, freshly arranged and pretty to behold. She smiled uncertainly and again Tabitha felt for her sister. It should have been her who lived cloistered and untouched, learning the ways of old. But Tabitha was not made for the maturity and ancient revered knowledge of Spellspeak. Wasn't she about to prove that now? Technically Brenton was not hers and had not lain with her, though they had both reached climax in each other's company. But who wanted to quibble about technicalities when the solution was so easily at hand?

The large kitchen of the old house was modern in conveniences such as a refrigerator and gas stove, but it also had a large pantry with a sliding panel leading to a staircase down to the partitioned cellar. Here Grandmother approached a large cabinet that was locked by no metal key. The cabinet was dark wood, old and worn, but free of wormholes and solid as it had stood for centuries, transported from another country, handed down from chosen ancestor to chosen ancestor. One day the cabinet would belong to Seline but for now it was strictly Grandmother's. The scrollwork hand-carved in the wood showed different animals changing forms. A dove became a hawk, a dog a wolf, a snake an alligator; like some fanciful evolution, and well it might have been except for the cat deeply etched in the wood changing into a person.

Near the center of the cabinet stood two indentations, shaped like palms. No one would ever understand how the cabinet could distinguish one print from another but a hundred different hands could press against these prints and the cabinet would stay sealed. But when Grandmother pressed her hands into these molds just as her predecessor had, the cabinet released its hidden catch and clicked open. When Grandmother passed on, the cabinet would then only recognize Seline as its mistress and would hide its secrets from all others. So it would be for many generations to come, unless Seline passed on without a direct female descendant.

Tabitha waited patiently as the cabinet slowly swung open without a creak of ancient wood. Curiously, Tabitha tried to see around Grandmother and inside the gaping door, but except for a few empty clear vessels, the other flagons and phials were murkily opaque or colored and did not seem to have any labels disclosing the contents. Grandmother, despite her years, seemed to know what was what as she hummed and passed her hand around, caressing some oddly shaped embossed flasks and murmuring to others, like precious offspring to be coddled with assuring words. "Ah, here we are." The older woman sighed contentedly.

A small bottle with pewter mounts was produced that held what looked like innocuously clear liquid inside. Tabitha held out her hand reverently, but Grandmother only chuckled. "No, my dear. Oh, no! Even this minute quantity would be the death of you. Death by..." Grandmother seemed to recall she was talking to her granddaughter and blushed slightly. "Well, just you never mind. It would be pleasant the first fifty times in succession, but copulating a thousand times, nonstop, despite pain and agony... No, you see why some things should never fall into untrained hands. Imagine if someone were to put this into the city's water supply! Gads, people like dogs, rutting in the streets. Night and day, nonstop. It doesn't bear thinking on." But her grandmother must have been contemplating the sight as she paused eloquently. "Where is that Phoenician vessel with the golden stopper? Ah, there my lovely. Come to Gram."

A tiny phial no bigger than Tabitha's pinkie was produced and a dropper measured out ten drops. The golden stopper sealed the vessel. "Now it's two drops for you and two for him. No more for the first dose, or I cannot be held accountable for the side effects on either of you! You both must take it or it has no effect. The pheromone-like reaction calls one mate to another exclusively, but beware...it is not always conducive to time and place. What I mean is as long as you are in the same room together..."

"We could be arrested for indecent exposure?"

"To say the least," Grandmother cautioned. "You remember the dogs rutting in the streets scenario?"

"Grandmother! Like I would allow that!" Tabitha scoffed.

"Oh, allow it you would. You would kill for it. Considered yourself warned." The older lady looked stern.

"Yes, ma'am," Tabitha replied dutifully. "Two drops for me and two for him."

"Yes. For the first dose. After two weeks you must administer a booster dose of two more drops each and then a month later, one drop each. Mix it in whatever liquid you wish. It takes twelve hours exactly, no matter the person's metabolism, for the first dose to take effect. It is an exact science. But it is not to be taken lightly. You must be certain he is the one you want, child. The aftereffects are primitive and not for the faint of heart. He will want you and only you. In all ways."

"Forever?"

"Follow the prescribed treatment plan and you will have his heart and body until you release him from the spell. Then if your love is true he will love you for all eternity."

"Eternity? But what if our love isn't everlasting and I want to break the spell? How?"

"No. I will not reveal the Sever Spell. It would be too easy to take this contract lightly if you knew how to break it on a whim. It is an involved process nonetheless. Think on it a day or so before you enter into a commitment that is unlike anything you have ever experienced. You are no longer an impulsive child, Tabitha. Think wisely before setting these events into motion. And follow my words precisely for the alternative is beyond your comprehension."

"Yes, Grandmother."

"Now go on up and bid your sister goodbye. I have some work to do down here, yet."

"Goodbye, Grandmother. I'm sorry I could not..." The guilt welled forth and Tabitha could not finish the sentence. Would she ever be able to visit her grandmother without these oppressive feelings?

"Your sister Seline is a fine apprentice. You were not meant to be alone and confined. I can see that now. Goodbye, my dear."

Her grandmother was already humming to her potions and phials and Tabitha knew she had been dismissed. Back in the kitchen her sister waited.

"You are going?" Seline questioned.

"Yes. I must. Are you very lonely here with just Grandmother?"

"No."

But Tabitha knew Seline was lying. "I'm sorry. I know it should be me here, alone and secluded."

"No, it shouldn't, so stop apologizing. It is my destiny. Besides, I am not alone, always. Gram allows me to visit Mother, and our incorrigible brother Tom comes and goes as he chooses. I think even Gram has fallen under his charm spell."

Tabitha chuckled. "It figures. Tom can wrangle his way into any woman's heart. I can't wait for the day when he meets his match."

Seline nodded agreement, then whispered, "I am to begin attending the covens very soon. Then I will be initiated."

"Aren't you frightened?"

"No. Though Gram won't tell me what is to happen, I know I must remain pure until I am thirty so it can't be too invasive."

Tabitha wished she could reassure Seline, but the truth was she did not know what happened at the coven initiations. No one outside the circle knew. And it was forbidden to be revealed. Unable to offer comfort she bade her sister farewell and hugging the phial of precious liquid, folded herself into her Miata and drove back to the hotel.

Chapter Four

Tabitha took the elevator up to her room humming softly to herself. She was getting antsy to try her plan out. Anticipation was her worst enemy. A sudden jolt to her nerves could make her transform unconsciously. She smiled at Davey as he commented on her good mood on the ride up and pressed her floor button.

When she opened the door to her room her senses began to tingle. Someone had been there and it wasn't the maid service. Tabitha knew their smell just as she knew the scent that wafted to her as soon as she entered her room.

Brenton had been there as sure as Tabitha breathed. But why? The room was empty now, but judging from the fading odor of his male scent mingling with Tuscany cologne spread throughout the suite, he'd not confined his presence to just the chair by the window, as he would have if he'd been sitting, waiting for her to return. The scent was strongest by the bed. Tabitha's nose twitched. He'd touched the mattress. She smelled his finger oil residue, invisible to any but the sharpest of animal noses, both on the bed sheet and the mattress.

Why in the world would he even be in her room? He'd never come there before. Always Tabitha reported to him. There was no note, nothing to indicate he wanted to see her. Nor that he had been there at all. If it weren't for her extraordinary sense of smell Tabitha wouldn't have known she'd had a visitor.

She frowned as she placed the phial of potion carefully on the dresser. Twelve hours until it would take effect. She would take hers now in a glass of water, then she would find Brenton and find a way to administer his. Twelve hours would be the early morning, purrfect for Tabitha's libido and metabolism. A rush of warm wetness pooled at the juncture of her thighs. She was going to find out things about Brenton and this sex thing that would make all the years of waiting worth it. And maybe if she could spare her tongue for other things, she would ask Brenton why he had been in her room.

Tabitha stripped and took a warm shower. It took all her willpower not to touch herself and bring about the release she habitually craved ever since she had met Brenton, but she wanted it all saved for him and their passionate encounter. She wasn't sure how the potion worked but she had an idea it caused both her and Brenton to release a pheromone compound that their basic chemistry recognized on each other and no one else was aware of. And she wanted to make sure everything was perfect for their tryst.

Wrapped in a towel Tabitha took up the potion and uncapped the golden cork. She couldn't help sniffing the phial. Nothing. No odor, not even a faint trace. Maybe it wasn't potent any longer. There was no telling how old it was. Probably centuries as Grandmother had once told her some things in the locked cabinet were irreplaceable. She placed a drop on her finger and licked it. No taste.

Well she would just make sure if it had lost its potency to take a precaution and double the dose. So instead of two drops she dripped four into a glass of cool water and drank it down. Even if the potion was at full potency what harm could two minute extra drops do? And she could always get more from Grandmother to complete the treatment.

She felt fine so she transformed and groomed herself to perfection before taking a short nap before dinnertime. At four she dressed with a vengeance, choosing a body-conscious ribbed knit dress in periwinkle that looked sensational with her dark auburn hair, styled in sexy disarray. The platinum and black high-heeled pumps shaped her legs provocatively. This would be Brenton's last chance to redeem himself and save his fate at the hands of the potion.

Tabitha took the phial and tucked it securely inside her small buttery soft clutch purse. She wondered if Brenton was *busy* that evening. No matter if he was. She would simply find a way to administer the potion then be on her way. In twelve hours he would be all hers...cock, stock and barrel.

This time when she took the elevator up to the penthouse she had the satisfaction of seeing Davey's eyes open wide at her choice of outfits and he whistled appreciatively. "You look wonderful, Ms. Fenwick. You must have big plans this evening."

Tabitha smiled sweetly, "The biggest, Davey. Did you take anyone else up to Brenton's...uh, Mr. Calder's this evening?"

"Oh, no, ma'am. He's been up there alone, all day."

"Really?" Tabitha thought that odd since she knew for a fact, he'd been in her room sometime earlier that day. Perhaps he'd taken the stairs. But why? Unless he didn't want to be seen. This was most curious.

She used her passkey but it didn't open Brenton's door. He'd had the code changed and even her master key wouldn't open it! Another enigma. She knocked softly, fighting the urge to kick the door soundly. She was not a patient female or feline.

Brenton called out, "Who is it?" His voice was muffled through the door.

What was this nonsense? Why was Brenton exercising such caution? "It's Tabitha."

The door was opened and looking almost relieved Brenton smiled down at her. "Tabitha, you're back! You were gone almost all day."

"No. I've been back a few hours." Her heart did a funny leap. Was he really glad to see her? His sexy half-smile said he was. Maybe the potion wasn't going to be needed…if she was reading Brenton's signals right.

"Didn't you get the message I left at the front desk that I wanted to see you?" Brenton looked irritated and the smile was gone. "Maybe I should get you a beeper."

Tabitha resented his tone. She was not a dog to be called to his side. She was dying to say, "Yes, *I* got the message but chose to ignore it." But she resisted the impulse to further irritate him and chose the truth. "No. I was given no message." Then to bait him she continued, "But you could have left one in my room, just to be sure I received it."

"No. I don't go into my employees' rooms. It doesn't look right."

Tabitha tilted her head. He was lying, covering his tracks.

He continued, "Anyway, you're here now, so it doesn't matter. Have dinner with me, will you? We need to talk business." He seemed to notice her appearance for the first time, but only glanced at her dress in a cursory appraisal. "Unless you have other plans?"

"No. I have all evening," Tabitha purred. *And I'll have you very soon.* The fact he hadn't even had the inclination to flirt with her by telling her she looked nice sealed his fate. *In twelve hours you're going to want me so bad, you'll be screaming how good I look underneath you. If I let you be on top.*

"Good. I just now ordered from room service. Go ahead and call and add yours on. I was just dressing."

Tabitha noticed his very expensive Enrico Venturi golden tan shirt was misbuttoned, as if he'd hurriedly donned it without stopping to check his appearance in the floor-length mirror he kept for that very purpose. This distraction was most out of character with her boss. Likewise, there was a wrinkle in the usually crisp espresso shaded, creased trousers he wore, and he was barefoot.

As Brenton disappeared back in the bedroom Tabitha called, "Do you have any wine?"

"In the fridge," he yelled back.

Tabitha found an open bottle of white zinfandel. She didn't even warrant an unopened bottle of expensive champagne such as Brenton lavished on his tall blonde companions he ritually kept company with. Without remorse Tabitha found two Baccarat crystal wineglasses and poured the zinfandel. She only poured a small amount into Brenton's to ensure he would consume the whole dose. Then she added two drops of the potion, then two more. Then remembering the trouble she had gone through to look attractive for him and he hadn't even noticed, Tabitha emptied the last of the potion into his glass.

Without compunction, she ordered braised chicken with creamed mushroom sauce from room service and charged it to Brenton's guest tab. When Brenton joined her, he was properly clad, his feet stuffed into a pair of brown Ferragamo loafers and his sandy hair combed back and styled into place. The delicious smell of Tuscany drifted from his person.

Tabitha casually handed him his glass, as without a word he took a generous swallow. Tabitha watched him closely, but the potion must truly not have had any taste. Brenton took another swallow and drained the glass without comment.

They sat at the Louis XV dining table and ate their dinners after room service delivered them. Brenton seemed to be more at ease but he drank a lot of water and Tabitha too, found herself thirsty. As she sipped and tried not to gulp the cool liquid, Brenton casually remarked, "Too bad about Diamond Charlie."

Tabitha paused, her glass halfway to her lips. "What about him?"

"You haven't heard, then? He's dead."

"He was out of shape and begging for a coronary with all the junk food he ate. I'm not surprised." Tabitha shrugged without sympathy.

"He fell twenty floors from the Granada Hotel balcony across town," Brenton answered, his tone gruff. "I don't think high cholesterol contributed to his death."

"Someone must have caught him in the act of thievery and decided to finish him off," Tabitha reasoned.

"Yeah," was all Brenton replied. He sipped his water slowly, then hurried on, "When you were in his room and retrieved Agatha Winters necklace, you didn't happen to find anything else, did you?"

"Like what?" Tabitha hedged.

"Like anything else. It's a simple question, Tabitha. Yes or no." His tone was low and forceful.

"He had some glow in the dark condoms and leather toys in the bedside drawer. You interested in those?" Tabitha teased. "I didn't take you for a kinky man but you never know what secrets people hide." Tabitha wished she had taken the sex toys. They might come in handy in a little less than twelve hours. *If* the potion worked and it was a very big *if*.

Tabitha figured she should be feeling something, extra body heat, the urge to rub up against Brenton and feel how hard he was. That was, if she excited him, which so far didn't seem to be the case as he was regarding her intently but with less passion than a bowl of fruit.

"Tabitha, it's important. Did you help yourself to anything else?" He was half out of his chair and reached with a snake's speed to grab her wrist in an iron clasp.

"What's the big deal? Charlie steals from others, so I stole from him."

"What did you take?" Brenton's voice was low and deadly.

Tabitha pulled her wrist but he didn't release his grip. Instead he came around to her side of the table and pulled her to her feet. "Where is it?" His tone would brook no argument.

"It was only some cash. Nine thousand dollars. Chump change to Charlie." Tabitha tried to pry his grip from her wrist but it was clamped like a vise.

"Where's the money now?"

"It's not in my room, as you well know!" She narrowed her eyes.

He had the grace to look uneasy before answering. "You are an employee and I can't condone thievery. You have to give me the money."

"The hell I do! If Diamond Charlie is dead then the money has no way to be traced. It's mine, or rather charity's."

"You gave the nine thousand to a charity?"

"Not yet. But I'm going to."

"I can't let you do that." Brenton sounded definite.

"Since when do you care about a measly nine thousand dollars that a two-bit thief stole in the first place? And you changed your door combo. What's going on, Brenton?"

"I can't tell you that either. Where is the money?"

"It's safe. And that's where it will stay until you tell me what's going on."

At the assurance that the money was still in her possession Brenton loosened his hold on her wrist. A bright red weal appeared. Almost ashamed, he rubbed at it, his fingertips brushing against her skin.

Tabitha watched his motions, wanting him to lick the weal, then continue to lick her whole body until she cried for more of what she had experienced earlier that week. She wanted to sink down to the floor and hike up her dress so Brenton could see her naturally burgundy bush and her equally alluring pussy that begged to be petted and stroked. Maybe the potion was working or maybe Tabitha was just horny for her chosen one to take her and penetrate her every which way imaginable.

But Brenton dropped her wrist and stepped back. "Is the money here in the Arpel?"

"No. But it's safe," she repeated.

"Tomorrow you will take me to it."

"Not unless you tell me why and if it has something to do with Diamond Charlie's 200 foot drop."

"Tabitha, I can't tell you that. It would be too dangerous. You have to trust me."

"No, I don't." Seeing he wasn't about to back down and knowing by tomorrow if the potion worked, the money would be the last thing on his mind, Tabitha suddenly acquiesced. "All right. Tomorrow, I'll take you to the money."

He took her at her word and looked relieved. His face took on the easygoing smile she was accustomed to. "I'll replace the money, if it makes you happy to give it to charity. Fine. Just not *that* money."

Tabitha shrugged. It was no matter to her. But the fact that it was so important to him that he would search her room and lie about it was intriguing. "Can I go now? I have some work-related things to do since I took today off."

He looked disappointed and Tabitha watched him scan over her shapely form in the body-hugging dress. Finally, she was getting some appreciation.

But his tone was all business. "Of course. I'll expect you here at nine in the morning. We'll go together to retrieve the money."

Tabitha only smiled. He would see her hours before that for other reasons.

* * * * *

Tabitha spent the rest of the evening preparing for what was to be the most memorable of her sexual life. She set out her black lace Victoria's Secret teddy and made plans to order a bottle of champagne and fresh strawberries, despite the early morning hours they would be requested. For Brenton, the hotel staff would jump as high as they were told, and catering to his requests was a requirement of employment.

Tabitha had planned on letting herself into Brenton's penthouse at 4 a.m. and sliding into his bed for a few lessons before ordering the champagne and strawberries. But since he had changed the combination and her pass card was invalid she would have to wake him up to be let in. She was counting on getting close enough to let the potion take effect, but just in case it didn't work, she had an excuse about being worried about the money, for visiting at such an unorthodox hour.

A little before four, Tabitha slid into the black lace teddy, resisting the urge to fondle her breasts through the lacy knit that stimulated her skin by mere touch. She looked good in black and knew it. A long camel-colored merino wool coat covered her modestly, even though Davey wouldn't be on duty and the elevator would be unattended at so early an hour. She still felt no different and was really beginning to think the potion was impotent. Damn! All the planning for nothing.

But she was already at Brenton's door and she could always just either use the money excuse or throw caution to the wind and discard the coat and jump on Brenton. He had been stressed earlier so perhaps her attentions would be welcome.

She knocked assuredly. There was only silence from within. She knocked harder but still no one stirred.

Frustrated, Tabitha kicked the door hard enough to wake even the most dedicated sleeper. Nothing. Tabitha tried the door and of course it was locked securely. She returned to her room and tried calling Brenton's emergency after-hours number. He didn't pick up. A sudden thought occurred to Tabitha. What if he'd had some sort of reaction to the potion and was lying unconscious inside his suite?

She controlled the impulse to overreact. It was about as useful as chasing her tail and not nearly as much fun. She calmed herself and thought about the next step. She called down at the desk and spoke to the night concierge. When had Mr. Calder last checked his messages? The concierge reported, not since yesterday afternoon but when he returned he would forward them.

Tabitha's ears perked up. Returned? Mr. Calder had left the hotel?

Maurice, the night concierge, was patient. Yes, he had gone out an hour ago with two men and said he would be gone for a few days on business. He left no message for Miss Fenwick and no indication exactly when he would return. Only…

Tabitha caught the hesitation in Maurice's usually monotone falsetto. "What?" she insisted.

Maurice had not liked the ilk of the men who accompanied Mr. Calder. They were not of his kind. They wore badly fitted suits and cheap cologne and reeked of cigars. Not the fine Cubans or Monacos, but the fat stogies found at the racetrack. Not to mention showing up at such an uncivilized hour and demanding access to Mr. Calder's rooms. Tabitha could picture Maurice's delicate nostrils flaring with disdain. Of course, he, Maurice, called up to Mr. Calder's suite and to his surprise Mr. Calder had told

Maurice to send up the men. Soon after they had all left together.

Tabitha pondered on this after she had hung up. What the devil was going on with Brenton? He had acted like recouping the nine thousand dollars was the end-all of priorities and now he had simply left without notice. It was most peculiar. Tabitha smelled a rat and not the four-legged variety!

There was no other recourse. She had to get into his suite and look around. Maybe he had left a note, forgetting she didn't have a new key for his rooms. Or at the very least, perhaps he had left a clue for her. She definitely needed to do some prowling around. Before she hung up she asked Maurice if Mr. Calder had left a key copy for her at the desk. No?

Well, Brenton was either under duress or something had come up that preceded the importance of the money. At least he didn't appear to be ill from the potion. It really must have been impotent. Well, that was something to take up with Grandmother after this Brenton mystery was solved.

It didn't take long for Tabitha to hatch her next plan of action. She headed back up to the penthouse. She didn't want to cause a ruckus by breaking the door in, but for her of course there was always another way.

Tucked in an out of the way corner of the penthouse hall was a small walk-in supply closet. Since only Brenton and a handful of staff were allowed in the penthouse, this was left unlocked. It contained an assortment of mops, brooms and cleaning supplies.

When Tabitha opened the door the pungent sharp aroma of Pine-Sol and lemony cleaner assailed her nostrils causing her to wince as her magnified sense of smell committed suicide and a sharp pain went through her sinus. She resisted the urge to take off running down the hall to escape the awful cacophony that raced through her body. Cleaning solvents were about as appealing as cat litter and were tantamount to sniffing glue. She tried not to twitch, knowing that was pure cat instinct and fought it down.

In the corner of the supply closet was a ladder for reaching high places and a small toolbox with a hammer and assorted size screwdrivers. And most important, high above in the ceiling was the air conditioning and heating vent. Using the ladder to reach, Tabitha unswiveled the two screws holding the vent in place with a Phillips screwdriver. Then perched on the ladder she transformed and jumped into the crawlspace.

Ugh, the dust and grime were despicable! Brenton had better appreciate this extra effort she was going to on his behalf. Never mind she had tried to drug him earlier that evening. That was beside the point. And what was really annoying was the fact she and Brenton should have been chasing each other around the room, hitting the sheets and doing to each other wonderfully mystical and flagrantly sexual things! Instead, Tabitha was crawling through a passageway of corrugated metal that was as cold as it was uninviting and creaky.

Tabitha came to the first vent in the penthouse suite's ceiling. Her elliptical pupils peered through the slats of the vent. Living room vent. Odd, all the lights were on in the room. She wanted the bedroom so she could jump down onto the nice soft bed. She kept going, glad of her small feline body that could maneuver easily in the compact space. When she reached the next vent she spied the king-size bed to the right, below. It would be an easy jump. But, the one thing Tabitha had forgotten was the screws on the outside of the vent. In her feline form she lacked the strength to dislodge the grill.

Damn, she'd have to transfer to human form inside the duct. Ooh, it was going to be a tight fit! She growled as she changed, her hips wedging uncomfortably against the vent sides. She hated being dirty and this was nothing short of grungy! Never mind she was naked, as her clothes had slid to the floor of the supply closet when she changed into cat form. Her skin was streaked with dirt and a filmy oily substance from the corrugated metal. Her annoyance gave extra impetus to her punch as using the heel of her hand she crunched into the vent. It popped off and fell to the floor below; the screws flying in all directions as the soft ceiling fittings gave way.

Tabitha launched herself out of the vent and bounced in human form onto the bed. The smell of Brenton rose from the covers reminding Tabitha of what she was missing. He'd better have a good excuse for this. Tabitha looked around the bedroom. The lights were on here as well. If Brenton had planned to be gone for a few days wouldn't he have shut off the lights?

Tabitha padded to the George III mahogany tallboy and standing on her tiptoes peeked inside the top drawers. Black and white Hugo Boss briefs were neatly folded inside along with rows of Calvin Klein socks in every shade of the rainbow and then some. One by one she pulled open drawers. Enrico Venturi dress shirts in bold dark colors and pastels neatly folded in tissue paper, as if just back from the cleaners, caught her eye. Crisp white Trussardi shirts that would need steaming to keep them wrinkle-free were stacked lovingly within. If anything was missing, it wasn't in quantity as the drawers were all full.

Tabitha entered Brenton's temple of worship—his cedar paneled, built to specification, walk-in closet. Racks of dark Valenti and Canali cashmere and wool suits hung neatly like soldiers at inanimate attention. Brenton's charcoal Emilio Yuste from Spain was in attendance as well as his Gianfranco Rossi gray sharkskin imported from Italy. On the opposite wall were the more informal pieces of Brenton's stylish wardrobe; his Marc Jacobs denim-washed jeans and rust-colored tweed Zegna sportcoat and the only item Tabitha didn't care for on Brenton, a houndstooth cashmere coat.

A revolving rack held Versace, Armani and Charvet ties. A similar rack displayed DKNY, Baltazar and Brenton's favored Versace Medusa Belt. Cubbyhole shoe shelves held Cole Haan croc slip-ons, Prada loafers and Gucci dress shoes in various colors. But the most alarming item of all was hanging front and center, a walnut brown Zegna rich napa leather jacket.

Brenton never left that jacket behind when he went out. Ever! He swore he wanted to be buried in that jacket no matter if it went with whatever else he was wearing. And for a clotheshorse like Brenton, that was a bold statement. What the hell was going on?

Tabitha left the closet almost reverently. Her danger senses were twitching on overkill. She spotted the golden tan Venturi shirt Brenton had been wearing when she had last seen him, thrown in a pile at the foot of the bed, carelessly as if he couldn't be bothered before selecting another shirt. Now that was just like Brenton. He must have been in the process of changing clothes when Maurice had called up about his two visitors, then for whatever reason he had changed his mind and just left as is. Nothing seemed out of place in the suite and there were no signs of a struggle. Odd, Brenton's cell phone was lying on the nightstand by the bed. He always took it with him, wherever he went, day or night.

Thinking practically, Tabitha donned the tan shirt to cover her nakedness and leaving the vent panel on the floor, she went through the rooms and turned off the lights before exiting through the front door. As she clicked the door closed behind her the gleam of metal caught her eye in the large potted Neanthe Bella palm next to the entryway of the suite. On closer inspection it turned out to be Brenton's TAG Heuer chronograph watch, the expensive timepiece tossed haphazardly or dropped into the palm. Nothing about this made any sense.

Tabitha retrieved the watch and grabbed her clothes from the supply closet before returning to her room. She couldn't stand the grime and oil on her person and spent the better half of an hour scrubbing herself clean in the shower. As dawn broke over the eastern sky Tabitha curled up on the bed, but sleep was elusive. The shirt of Brenton's lay at the foot of the bed and Tabitha could still vaguely detect his scent on it even from that distance. She retrieved the shirt and cradled it to her, the spicy amber and cinnamon smell of Tuscany and Brenton's own manly scent comforted her as she fell into an uneasy slumber wondering — where was Brenton?

Chapter Five

She couldn't have slept for long as she awoke hot and clammy, too uncomfortable to ignore. Her breasts tingled, as she lay naked on top of the covers with only Brenton's shirt covering her partially. In her sleep she must have rolled it on top of her. But why was she burning up? The soft silky material was in no way thick enough to keep her warm, nonetheless a raging inferno.

She sat up and the shirt fell to her waist. It touched off a trail of sparks as it tumbled to her lap and landed across the top of her pubis. The heat was building again and now it centered in her *mons*. How much heat could she stand? she wondered, as suddenly a shaft of white-hot pain sent her shooting backward to lie prone again on the bed. The pain eased to a pleasant tingling inside her cunt that reflexively made her clench and release her vaginal muscles as if gripping a cock in the act of sex. The tingling became an electric sensation that made her whole body vibrate as if a dildo were inside her pulsing and making her shake in anticipation.

The sleeve of Brenton's shirt fell onto Tabitha's labia and she screamed in a sudden orgasm that shook her from head to toe. The fire was not assuaged however and Tabitha writhed in agony of a sexual nature that begged for release. God, it felt so bad, yet so good! She must do something! Her hand grasped the shirt and she tried to move it aside to touch herself. But the shirt clung insidiously to her nether lips, seeming to feed from her.

Tabitha grasped the other sleeve and brought it down, sliding it between her musky folds. The tingling began again. She worked the sleeve back and forth, seesawing it against her cleft. The heat began to intensify and she pushed the cuff inside her.

Of its own volition her cunt contracted around the material and began to spasm in rapid succession. In her mind the shirt became a cock, soft as silk yet hard as a pulsing rocket invading her inner recesses, insistent and welcome but invasive and trespassing all at the same time. Tabitha didn't want her contact with Brenton to be in this surrogate way but she was helpless to stop the impulse that drove her on. She swore it was Brenton's cock hitting her womb as she shot upward to a sitting position and screamed with an orgasm that washed from her head to her toes and caused a gush of liquid to flow from her onto the shirt.

Panting, Tabitha stared around her empty room. Had she been dreaming? The shirt was still half inside her, resting against her thighs. To her shock the burning was starting again. Tabitha grabbed the shirt and flung it off her body. Within seconds the heat dissipated and Tabitha was left in a state of post-coital bemusement, ashamed she had experienced an orgasm that left her former attempts at self-fulfillment far behind, yet she was alone and only Brenton's shirt had brought about the reaction. What the hell was going on?

There would be no further sleep for Tabitha and she rolled sluggishly out of bed, her limbs leaden and weighted down. Despite her two orgasms she still felt unfulfilled and irritable. There had been physical release but mentally she was wound as tight as a spring as if she had been merely teased. The eruption of orgasm was only skin deep and her soul still hungered with an emptiness that demanded to be assuaged. It was a feeling Tabitha compared to walking on an electrified tightrope that shocked you for walking yet you didn't dare fall and were forced to endure the discomfort.

The weak morning light indicated a heavy cloud layer as Tabitha showered and dressed in sage pleated pants and a coral knit tunic that highlighted her hair vividly. She contemplated her next move over cold cereal with whole milk. She more or less played with the cereal and lapped up the milk but she wasn't very hungry only wanted to avoid a noisy complaining stomach.

She walked through the hotel on her rounds, checking in at the front desk. Brenton hadn't called or left any messages. Every little noise caused Tabitha to start and she knew if she were in cat form her hair would be standing on end. All her instincts told her something was wrong but she had no proof to call the police, and trying to convince them her feline senses were right 99.9 percent of the time would only get her time in the loony bin so she spent the day restless and pacing. By late afternoon, unable to nap, she had to get out for some fresh air or she'd scream! As she passed the front desk, the new day concierge, a buxom blonde named Suzy, who Tabitha knew Brenton had personally hired, called out to her.

"Ms. Fenwick?"

Tabitha turned and arched an eyebrow in inquiry.

"A message just came in from Brenton. He asks that you meet him across the street in front of the Gina Mia Restaurant at 5:00."

Tabitha disliked the familiarity of Suzy calling Brenton by his first name, but Brenton insisted all his employees drop protocol. Tabitha entertained no such rule and liked to be addressed as Ms. Fenwick, especially by Brenton's jelly bean sweetie. "Did he say anything else?"

"No. Only that, then he hung up before I could even say goodbye."

Tabitha frowned. She didn't feel any better about the message. Would Suzy even know if it were really Brenton calling, or would she take the caller at his word? But it was a risk Tabitha would have to take. She had no choice. If Brenton was in danger she needed to find out from whom and so far this was her only lead. She looked at her dependable Timex strapped to her wrist. Four-fifty. The Gina Mia was just a stone's throw away. She'd get to the restaurant a few minutes early and scout around. Maybe she would see something or someone until either Brenton, or whoever had called, showed up.

Tabitha was almost out the door when she heard Suzy call her back. "Ms. Fenwick, it's Brenton. Oh, he's hung up again!"

Tabitha was developing a headache and irritably called, "What did he say?"

"He wants you to meet him at Casey O'Malley's Pub at five instead."

Tabitha swore under her breath. Casey O'Malley's was no stone's throw distance, but rather in an older part of town frequented by a rough crowd. Tabitha was no alley cat and did not relish going there alone at dusk. And there was no way to be there on time. Damn Brenton! What was his game?

She took a cab to the old factory district and had the driver park across the street from O'Malley's so she could size the place up. The grizzled, unshaven taxi driver looked at Tabitha's small person and asked, "You sure this is where you want to be dropped, lady? This ain't no tearoom, ya know?"

"Believe me, it's not my idea of a good time," Tabitha muttered as she paid the driver.

She started to ask him to wait but the cab driver must have read her mind. "Sorry toots, a parked cab in this part of town is a sitting duck. You're on your own. Got a cell phone?"

Tabitha shook her head. Damn, why hadn't she brought Brenton's cell? It wasn't as if it were doing any good sitting on his nightstand. But she gingerly stepped from the cab into the gloomy dusk, observing as a few roughnecks crossed the street in mid-block, not caring if the word jaywalking applied or not. She watched as the cab drove off then waited to cross as a car drove by.

Tabitha's feline instinct was to run in front of car headlights. They drew her like a moth to a flame and she always had to fight the urge to commit near suicide. It was a definite cat thing and one that defied logic. Usually she was able to bite her lip to keep her mind sidetracked and the urge held at bay. This evening she waited on pins and needles and after the car went by she started across the street. She became aware of three things at once...the smell of an acrid cigar, the sound of footsteps behind her and the sound of a car engine being gunned.

Out of the gloom a dark sedan screeched as its tires spun on blacktop, gripping the pavement and shooting forward, its headlights off and heading with deadly intent straight for Tabitha. The lack of headlights worked in Tabitha's favor, as they couldn't mesmerize her into freezing. With the reflexes of a cat Tabitha sprinted forward and the car fender just missed her.

The footsteps behind Tabitha were gone and she hastily looked about but whoever had been behind her was nowhere in sight. But Tabitha's eyes had seen one thing as certain as she was standing living and breathing on the sidewalk outside Casey O'Malley's. The face of the car's driver was as familiar as the back of her paw. It had been Brenton sitting behind the wheel, his handsome face contorted in hatred. Brenton had tried to run her down!

* * * * *

Tabitha's nerves were frayed and she wanted to pounce on someone to relieve her anger. There wasn't much sense in visiting Casey O'Malley's when the man she was to meet was trying to kill her but Tabitha could certainly use a drink.

The interior of the pub was a mixture of stale whiskey and the glow of neon beer signs. Tabitha's sensitive nostrils did a double dive, as she smelled body odor and cheap cologne as thick as Vaseline. The few women in the place were pros and Tabitha stuck out like a sore thumb. She wasn't sure what angered her more, Brenton for suggesting this place, or for trying to run her down. Either way, all thoughts of hot sex with Brenton were erased and she only wanted revenge and a piece of his hide.

Tabitha ordered a Kahlua and crème and nursed the drink from a dark corner where she could see without being seen. She had no intention of dodging drunken lewd proposals all night but safety in numbers seemed to be a wise choice. The bar's clientele favored blue-collar workers, some from the docks and some from the warehouses that lined the back alleys of this part of town. For the most part they seemed cut from the same cloth; heavy canvas clothing or coveralls and wool knit caps or bare-headed with coarse features from a hard life and harder drinking.

Tabitha stood with her back to the dingy plaster-flaked wall. From behind her she heard a rustling noise through the thin wallboard then a husky voice, "How do you want it?"

A man's low tone answered, "Straight fuck and talk dirty. I like that."

A thump against the wall sounded then as pounding began, the vibrations building into a rhythm, "Yeah, shove it in me. You're sooo big. That's it. Ooh, slam it home big fella. Come on. Come on. You're the best I've ever had. So big. Fuck me. Fuck me. Make me come. Yeah baby…"

Tabitha rolled her eyes. The woman's tone was so false she was obviously a pro making her living. The sound and noise were a play-by-play that Tabitha didn't need to witness to know what was going on. But it did nothing to arouse her the way Brenton had. Damn, him! Why did he have to turn out to be a louse and try and kill her? That was just plain rude!

A moment later a lady appeared from the back, her blouse half-undone and her breasts bulging from her push-up bra. Her red garish lipstick was smudged and the scent of sex came off her in waves. A man followed behind her, his pants unzipped and his dick partially visible. Tabitha watched the pair walk unsteadily towards the bar where one of the man's cronies must have pointed out his dangling peter as a sudden guffawing and raucous laughter broke out.

The acrid stench of a cheap stogie drifted to Tabitha and she recognized it as the same smell that she had noted right before the car had accelerated towards her. Not that quite a few of the pubs patrons didn't reek of tobacco but this was a peculiar odor, sour and sweet all in one. A particular brand, cheap but distinctive. The kind of smell that clung to everything it came in contact with, including the air.

Tabitha glanced to where the smell drifted from. Standing just inside the pub's doorway stood a man in a polyester-checkered suit. From his mouth protruded a stogie of obscene proportions. His features were a mass of wrinkles and lines mixed with pockmarks. His body frame was big, not fat but solid and pear-shaped. Tabitha's sharp eyes noted the man's own piggy gaze as he swept the room, trying for casual interest and failing miserably. He was looking for someone and Tabitha had an intuitive suspicion it was she. Her skin prickled with unease. The man was trouble; she sensed it with every fiber of her being.

Tabitha leaned back further in the shadows and considered her options. It seemed best to get out of the pub undetected and that meant transforming. Damn, she was fond of the soft tunic she wore and she would lose it in the process, but her life was more important. With a last sip of her drink Tabitha crouched down in the corner and stretched. Her skeleton made a few popping noises as it adjusted but in the noisy pub it went unnoticed, as did the small furry animal sidling through the crowd towards the door.

Tabitha paused behind a plastic plant in an urn that had seen better days. It now served as a spittoon for the pubs uncultured clientele. She was a hair's breath away from the stogie puffer in the cheap suit. He reeked strongly of bay rum and rancid breath. He didn't seem in any hurry to vacate his post in front of the door.

Further irritated that her evening had gone from bad to worse, Tabitha made an impulsive dash towards the man. She unsheathed her claws and in a flurry of movement ran up his leg straight for his groin. Her claws found their mark and dug in with a vengeance. The man howled with shock, obviously thinking a rodent from the docks had attacked him in the darkened pub, he yelled with terror. The pain in his dick and balls had to be excruciating as it radiated outward like a hot probe of agony, shooting through his groin, causing him to collapse in a heap screaming, "A rat. A rat bit my balls! For God's sake call an ambulance!" He shrieked in pain, "I think it bit off my dick. Someone do something! The pain…"

But it was too late. The crowd thinking he'd yelled the plural "rats" was a tide of shifting bodies trying to get out the door before the vicious rodents took over. No one in their right mind relished going through the series of rabies shots that were mandated for a rat bite and outside in the open air seemed the best antidote. Bodies stepped on and over the prostrate form lying on the floor, writhing in pain. No one noticed the small slinky form that raced through the door ahead of the crowd and disappeared across the street.

Tabitha had little choice but to remain in feline form and try to find a way back to the hotel. She couldn't very well transform into a naked human and hitch a ride. Likewise her purse was back at the pub with her clothes and she had no way to retrieve it. Her money was as good as gone as well as her clothes. She was in a pickle. She could have taken her car to the pub but at the time it hadn't seemed like a good idea as any car on this side of town was a vandal's dream.

She caught a ride in the back of a flatbed pickup headed back from the docks. At the intersection a few miles from the hotel, she spotted a shuttle bus and jumped onto the bumper, hanging on for dear life. As the bus passed the hotel Tabitha jumped off into the darkness, narrowly being missed by a taxicab pulling up to the Arpel hotel.

Now she was faced with an entirely different set of problems. The hotel doors were minded by a doorman as well as bellhops waiting to help with luggage. There was no way Tabitha could gain entrance that way. But there were alternate routes for savvy felines with inside knowledge of the hotel's workings.

Tabitha scooted around to the back of the hotel to the kitchen entrance. Damn! The doors were closed until deliveries in the morning. But further on, the basement windows were opened to let the steam from the laundry evaporate. Tabitha sighed, which came out a meow of sad proportions. The windows were easy to negotiate in her current form and she landed inside a room as steamy as a sauna with hot tumblers rotating towels to dry and hot presses going full steam.

A kind maid Tabitha recognized as Gabby caught sight of the red tabby cat meandering between noisy equipment and paused to murmur a few kind words, "Poor kitty. Are you a stray?"

Tabitha had always liked Gabby in her brief contact with the laundry maid, but Gabby's status in Tabitha's eyes was about to be promoted to adoration as Gabby scooped Tabitha up in her arms and stroked her soft fur. "Come with me, kitty. I'll bet we have some nice leftovers in the kitchen for you."

Tabitha purred with relief at being home and the thought of dinner made her knead her claws with happiness. True to her word Gabby poured a generous bowl of cream for Tabitha in the vast kitchen area of the hotel. She also found a platter of smoked salmon quiche and offered it to the feline, not sure if it was cat-digestible. But Tabitha's purr settled the issue as she delicately picked through the quiche eating the salmon bits until she was full. Then bless Gabby's heart she brought a large warm towel from the laundry and folded it for the tabby to lay on.

Tabitha didn't have the heart to refuse the kindness. She would just lie down for a few minutes until Gabby went back to work then she would find a way up to her room. *Just a few minutes*, Tabitha thought as she curled up on the toasty warm towel and drifted off in an exhausted sleep.

* * * * *

Tabitha woke sometime in the middle of the night. She was lying half on a towel and half on a hard cement floor and she was in human form, naked. Damn it! She had fallen asleep on the kitchen floor and transformed in her sleep. She sat up and moaned...the floor was hard as a rock and her body felt every bit of it.

Tabitha wrapped the towel around herself and tiptoed out to the back hall where a network of passages kept the staff of the Arpel out of public view as they did their menial duties. Using the freight elevator she reached her room unseen, retrieved a hidden pass card, and quickly let herself in. She headed straight for the shower, taking time to ease the stiffness and foul odors of the pub. One thing was on her mind, payback for her trouble. Brenton was going to get his and it wasn't going to be the pleasurable experience that Tabitha had planned for him.

When she was clean and groomed to perfection, Tabitha donned a pair of jeans and a nondescript pullover. She wanted another look at Brenton's suite, assuming he hadn't returned. She checked by phone at the front desk where Maurice was back on night duty. No messages from Brenton and he hadn't returned to Maurice's knowledge. Thankfully, Davey wasn't on duty as Tabitha rode up to the penthouse in the elevator.

There was no way Tabitha was going to dirty herself on Brenton's behalf crawling through the air vents again. Not a chance in hell! In the supply closet she rummaged through the small tool chest and emerged with a hammer and flat-edged screwdriver. Gentleness being the last thing from her mind Tabitha wedged the screwdriver in the doorframe in front of the mechanism and slammed it a few times with the hammer, almost humming with satisfaction as the violent action gave her temper an outlet. The mechanism snapped and the door clicked open, an ugly gash marring its smooth, polished surface. She hoped Brenton would be livid at the blatant vandalism.

The penthouse was dark and silent. It looked the same as Tabitha had left it. Brenton's bedroom still showed the ceiling vent missing and the pieces lying on the thick dark Berber carpet. Brenton's cell phone on the nightstand rang softly, more of a chirp. Tabitha grabbed it and looked at the small display window. Only the battery needing to be charged. The phone chirped again, reminding her of its fading power.

Startled, Tabitha almost dropped the small instrument as her turbo-charged nerves overcompensated and her quick reflexes responded. She literally twitched with irritation and indecision. She was about to toss the phone on the bed and leave when an idea struck her. She pressed the menu key on Brenton's cell and searched for the right buttons until his dialed calls appeared.

Using the cell's diminishing power she pressed send and dialed the last number Brenton had called, noting the time he'd placed the call. An answering machine picked up and gave a spiel about Regeant's Fine Imports and Furnishings. That wasn't especially odd as Brenton liked the finer things and could be doing business with the firm. But the time Brenton had placed the call was a little before three a.m., not too long before the two men in cheap suits had arrived and Brenton had disappeared. Now that did bear looking into.

Tabitha noted the address the recorded message had given for Regeant's was Cobble Street and Old Harbor Road. For an import business to be located near the docks wasn't unheard of, but was it a coincidence that Old Harbor Road was remarkably near Casey O'Malley's, the pub where Brenton had tried to run her down, and the awful man in the checkered suit and stinking stogie had turned up? Tabitha knew she was on to something. Her feline intuition was working overtime telling her it all was linked. But she also sensed more danger than just Brenton trying to run her down.

She would try to exercise caution though it went against her inherited instincts not to just drive over to the warehouse and slap someone around until they came up with some answers. Too bad she wasn't of the *Panthera onca* species, now that was a cat that could do some panther-sized damage! Sometimes it sucked being a runty tabby of the Felidaen subspecies.

Tabitha was about to throw the weakening cell phone onto the bed when she noticed something peculiar. Her fingers where they had touched the keypad were growing warmer. Curious, Tabitha sniffed her fingers and smelled just a trace of Brenton's scent where the oil from his fingers lingered on the keys and had transferred to Tabitha's own skin. She glanced at the phone in her hand, was it her imagination or was it growing warmer in her palm?

The phone looked innocuous enough but the LCD display suddenly lit up and the low battery words disappeared. It *was* becoming warmer in her hand. Tabitha peered closely at the display. The picture of two batteries appeared in the top right corner. The phone wasn't as low on juice as she had thought.

A sudden tingling in her fingers traveled into her hand and made her gasp. The phone's display glowed brighter and the third battery sign appeared. What the hell? The phone was charging itself.

There was a sudden twinge in Tabitha's cunt as a surge of electricity traveled down her arm to her nether regions. She swore the phone began to vibrate in her palm. Tabitha's knees weakened and she fell to a kneeling position. Of their own volition her hands traveled down to the crotch of her jeans and rubbed the phone against her *pubis*. A spasm shot through Tabitha like a blowtorch through ice. She was unable to help herself as she unzipped her jeans and moved aside her panties. She touched her clit and moved it back and forth but the heat wasn't enough. She eased the cell phone inside her underwear and pushed it against her labia. The fire shot through her unchecked and she rubbed the small vibrating cell against her cleft like a lover's fingers stroking her. She swore it was Brenton's long fingers encircling her, teasing her before inching their way inside her, inciting her to move with their to and fro motion.

She hated Brenton for trying to kill her, but God help her she'd do anything to have his cock pulsing inside her at this moment! To feel him pushing inside her, filling her with his girth and length, making her writhe and moan, pleading for him to fuck her.

A rush of thick secretion flowed from Tabitha's cunt, bringing her back to reality but she was helpless to stop the burning from within that drove her to work her clit mercilessly. She arched her back and screamed, a primal sound between a groan and a shriek, as if her soul were being torn from her body. She wanted to come so badly and she swore her blood pressure was rising by the second with the quickening of her breath. Her vaginal muscles clenched but as if discovering Brenton's cock was absent, Tabitha's whole body went cold and she shivered uncontrollably. Kneeling on the floor, no longer riding the cell phone as it pressed against her *mons*, she quivered like a bewildered idiot. The cell was cold now and emitted a low battery beep.

Tears gathered on her cheeks and she had no idea when she had started crying. She let herself fall back onto the soft, thick Berber carper and lay dazed, not knowing what had just occurred. After a few minutes the cell in her hand began to warm up and pulsed in her palm again. The LCD display was lit again and the batteries were recharging themselves.

Instinctively Tabitha knew she had to get rid of the phone to be free of its cursed lure. With viciousness born of shame and anger at her weakness, she heaved the phone against the bedroom wall, taking comfort in the sound of it cracking, pieces flying in all directions. Tabitha lay back with a relieved sigh.

Within moments her fingers began to burn with that tingling intensity that traveled down her arm and invaded her cunt, insidious and insistent that she touch herself, and rub herself into a frenzy. It had to be the aftermath of Brenton's skin oils from the phone pad, Tabitha realized, as she leapt to her feet and hiked up her jeans, rushing into Brenton's bathroom and hitting the tap knobs to full force. She lathered her hands several times and washed with scalding water, wincing as her skin took the brunt of the punishment.

The potion! Tabitha knew without a doubt whatever was happening had something to do with the potion. Anything that had come into contact with Brenton's body would send Tabitha into a sexual frenzy. And the delay time seemed to be in the realm of five minutes before the mania peaked again. Her grandmother had warned her to be careful and like an errant child Tabitha had not listened. Hadn't she rashly taken more potion than prescribed? Now just a touch of Brenton's skin oil or his scent would send Tabitha into a sexual high that could not be assuaged, no matter how much she touched, stroked or even fucked herself. Oh God, she couldn't even achieve orgasm! Only that hollow almost there, but can't be relieved frustration that made her want to yowl like a tomcat and tear into something.

What the hell was Tabitha going to do? The man who had tried to kill her was also the one she wanted to fuck her to death!

Chapter Six

Tabitha's other quandary should have been easy. Getting to the dock area and Regeant's Imports. But since her handbag had been left at Casey O'Malley's, so was all her cash...which meant no money for a cab. Likewise, it also meant no driver's license or car keys. There was one solution and Tabitha wouldn't have thought twice about using it, but for one factor.

Brenton had a car, a rather nice one. An Aston Martin Vanquish, mega-expensive and well-bred, if you were a millionaire with no cares about high-priced repair bills. Tabitha knew where the keys were. Brenton made no bones about flouting the sterling silver key ring with steel wings engraved prominently. But Brenton had touched that ring plenty of times and his scent and skin oils were bound to be all over it. And for Tabitha that meant unfulfilled sexual mania all over again. The answer was gloves. Tabitha needed gloves.

She found a pair of latex ones in the supply closet off the hall of the penthouse. The other problem was the car itself. Tabitha had no problem finding it in the garage under the hotel and she gingerly pressed the key ring and unlocked the door with a beep. The black leather seats were soft and buttery, made for comfort. Tabitha sighed. And Brenton's ass had been firmly planted in them plenty of times. Likewise, she couldn't chance her arms accidentally touching the steering column or resting anywhere Brenton had touched casually, marking the territory and making it a sex trap for Tabitha.

Sitting where Brenton had sat was definitely touch and go. Would her jeans alone offer enough protection? Tabitha was taking no chances and raced back to the room in the back of the garage basement where various electrical boxes and controls were housed. She found a pair of white overalls, greasy but of thick canvas and stepped into them, zipping them protectively. They were huge on her but they would work for the purpose she required.

Tabitha had one last problem; Brenton's scent was bound to be in the car and would waft to her. Tabitha could imagine herself getting pulled over, her hands fondling herself, trying to get herself off, like a rabid dog in heat while the policeman called for backup and the men in the white coats. No, she had better cover all bases.

The garage attendant wasn't on duty yet. Brenton had a pass card that raised the wooden gate to allow him to come and go as he pleased. Lou, the usual daytime attendant had bursitis in his shoulder. He constantly applied Ben Gay until he reeked of the stuff and the whole garage smelled of unguent. His booth was empty but open on the side. Tabitha found his supply of Ben Gay and rubbed a thick trail under her nose. She nearly had a hissy fit as her senses were assailed by the pungent odor and her eyes filled with tears. Damn Brenton for this! He was gonna pay big-time!

When she was sure of her reinforcement against any pheromone reaction Tabitha got behind the wheel, carefully adjusting the seat forward by electronic control, and eased out of the garage like some sort of germ freak. Her hands were encased in yellow latex, her body enveloped in white canvas. She looked like a reject from

Ghostbusters or a generic HazMat team member. Tabitha gritted her teeth, knowing how ridiculous she looked.

The last obstacle she would just have to acknowledge and ignore. Taking a car of this caliber to the docks was about as sensible as a woman going there alone in the dark was. But Tabitha was batting a million tonight so what the hell? Besides, it would be daylight in a few hours and the nighttime scum that used the docks for nefarious activities would crawl back into their holes and the day workers would be up and around.

Any other time Tabitha would have been able to judge how close she was to the docks by the tang of saltwater in the air and the smell of night fog drifting aimlessly in wisps, like ghosts in the darkness. But tonight all Tabitha smelled was Ben Gay and she hated it. She practically growled as she drove, wanting to shred the car's leather seats with her claws extended, over and over, taking out her frustrations and aggression. But she couldn't seek retribution until she knew what was going on. But she would get even, oh, yes she would!

If there was any trace of Brenton in the Vanquish, and Tabitha was positive there had to be, then she was safe, as she had no reaction, except a Ben Gay high as she drove. The traffic was light still, the morning rush a few hours away. The closer to the docks she got, the more sporadic the traffic as delivery trucks came and went and semis took over, looking to load, or unload cargo.

Old Harbor Road ambled around the oldest docking ports. Cobble Street was *the* oldest street known in the city as it got its name from the stones embedded in its surface and had existed since milk trucks were drawn by horses and cabbies tipped their hats.

Like most bygone era streets it was narrow and noisy, the car tires making a whomping noise as it eased over the cobbles. Tabitha followed Old Harbor until she came to Cobble and made a right. The ancient street had once fronted a booming fish and flower market but sometime during the Great Depression it had changed its caliber of people from regular working stiff to irregular business trade. Huge warehouses backed up to one side of Cobble Street and the fish market square was now a ghost town of rotting boards and homeless folk, living in the alleys and occasionally finding handouts or money-for-hire jobs at the docks.

To park Brenton's Vanquish on the narrow road was suicide for the car but Tabitha had other things to worry about. The warehouses were mostly brick and cement, their huge slab walls had writing of once prosperous businesses, long since relocated to a better part of town, or failed investment ventures, long since gone. None of these buildings had seen fresh paint since World War II and it was impossible from the angle to tell what was housed within. The physical address of Regeant's did not help as none of the buildings had numbered addresses. How did the place do any business? Maybe they didn't, not legal anyway.

Tabitha backed the Vanquish into an alley that had nothing to recommend it except dark shadows and anonymity. She certainly didn't want to cruise up and down looking for the right warehouse. She'd stick out to any passerby or person acting as lookout. There was a rustling sound coming from deep in the alley. Tabitha waited but no one appeared. Only a gust of wind or a homeless person restlessly lurching about in his makeshift cardboard box home. The street was eerie at this hour;

night not quite relinquishing its hold, and day not yet gaining its momentum.

As a token gesture Tabitha locked the Vanquish, the beep of the electronic remote lock echoed like a gun blast to the end of the alley, bouncing back. So much for subtlety, Tabitha thought wryly. She made her way to the old disused fish market, a faint odor of fish from days gone by still redolent in her nostrils. Or was it her imagination? Perhaps wishful thinking? The old wooden stalls were long gone, the lumber used for trashcan fires for the numerous street urchins and wandering alcoholic minstrels. Now only newspapers blew across the square, teased by the wind that scooted them like ghosts in a dance dependent on air currents.

A rat darted across the tamped dirt and chipped cement that comprised the ruined foundation of the square. Tabitha resisted the urge to chase it. Now was not the time. No benches remained from the original architectural design of a busy, predictable lifestyle with pigeons and seagulls swooping down for handouts. Now there was only Tabitha swooping in to find Brenton.

There were numerous passages leading from the market square meandering between the huge buildings. Some of these were wide enough for carts from the docks to bring in fresh catch for selling. The deep grooves in the dirt still gave credence to this even if it had been more than twenty years since the market was used. Tabitha chose a passage at random and crept between the brick and cement walls of the huge, hulking warehouses. These buildings had neither back entrances nor side doors as they used the docks at their front for loading and unloading. There was still no hint of what these monsters housed and Tabitha had little choice but to follow the passage through to where it met Old Harbor Road. At least here the buildings fronted the docks and had valid entrances.

As she turned the corner onto Old Harbor, a white van rumbled over the pitted road on its way to the docks. Tabitha resisted the urge to duck back down the passage. After all, she had a perfectly legitimate right to be on the street and it would have looked odd for her to skulk about in the shadows.

The first building was Charter Boats, a wholesale and repair shop where the smell of fiberglass and resin seeped from the pores of the bricks shoring up the decrepit edifice, as if the building oozed the thick compounds. Even with the Ben Gay under her nose, Tabitha picked up the sweet acidic odor and sneezed. She patted the pockets of her jeans and found a scrap of Kleenex that had actually made it through the wash and yet miraculously was slightly intact. With this Tabitha wiped her nose and tried to lose the Ben Gay ointment that was irritating the membranes and skin around her nose.

The next building had a royal blue awning that at one time had been a jaunty addition, but left neglected had been shredded to ribbons by the sea wind and salt air. This building had a whitewashed façade but no sign hanging or painted in sight. To further muddy the identity of the business, one of the large windows was boarded up and the other pane of glass was painted black. Tabitha shielded her eyes and tried to peer through the opaque paint, using her keen vision to cipher through the inky blackness. But it was no good and she couldn't make heads or tails what was inside.

Frustrated she checked the large front door. Not only was it also blackened with paint but a large chain and padlock was wrapped through the handle and anchored to a pole set in the front cement walkway. Tabitha looked up at the building, forlorn and cold in the early morning darkness. She would try the next building. Maybe she was barking up the wrong tree. She laughed at her choice of words.

The next building was clearly labeled The Oriental Dragon and showed statuary and paintings through the window. Fu dogs grinned malevolently in their ceramic green painted bodies, slashed with brilliant red. Folding screens, intricately painted with long-tailed feathered Phoenix and bonsai trees, sheltered part of the interior and no matter how she craned her neck Tabitha could see nothing more. But she did catch the glimmer of the gold letters on the glass, which also proclaimed The Oriental Dragon. They were stenciled over another group of words; the blurred edges where they had been ineffectually erased just barely visible. Regeant's had at one time been stenciled on the glass.

But why did a defunct business still have an active phone line? Had they relocated? Tabitha's instincts told her the answer to the puzzle lay within the building. She tried the door. It was locked tight of course. The other side fronted another passage leading back to the fish market. Tabitha paced back and forth considering her options.

On the side, high up in the brick wall of the building, was a vent propped open. Even in cat form it was doubtful Tabitha could jump half that distance but with a running jump, maybe. Her legs were awfully short for that height. But she really had little choice but to try.

She stretched her human body and dropped to all fours. She transformed quickly, crawling out of the pile of jeans, sweater and overalls. She would make a point of coming back for them. For one thing, she needed the protection of the coveralls for her drive back to the hotel and for another she was darn tired of losing her clothes and shoes over some no-good scoundrel by the name of Brenton Calder!

From her position on the ground the vent looked even more daunting of a distance. Tabitha backed up and took a running jump. Her springy legs propelled her almost a foot short of the window vent. She might be good for three leaps before she lost her momentum and her muscles tired.

Her second jump took her to the lip of the window and gave her hope. She backed way up and gave it a mad dash and half-ran half-leapt up the bricks, using their rough surface to help give her impetus. She reached the ledge of the vent frame and stuck both her front paws inside, clinging with her claws extended into the wood. By pulling herself up an inch, she could just barely see inside, but she couldn't hold herself for long.

With a growl she used her claws to scrabble for a better grip and pulled herself up. She was able to crawl through the vent but the inside of the warehouse was darker than outside and it took a moment for her pupils to adjust. From that height Tabitha could see a great deal. But beyond the folding screens were only pieces of ornately carved furniture, certainly nothing worth all the trouble she had endured.

She was about to jump back down, not relishing the painful jarring leap to the cement below when she heard a gentle whirring from a back corner of the cavernous warehouse. A reflection of yellow was briefly visible then the whirring noise and darkness again. Someone had come through a door from a lighted room then closed the door. There was the echo of hard-soled shoes then a flashlight beam was making its way towards the front of the building. Why didn't the occupant just turn on the lights? Unless they had something to hide. Tabitha waited and when she made out the pear-shaped individual passing below she could not contain her fierce growl. The reeking odor of a stogie filtered up to her. She found herself wishing for the Ben Gay to disguise the stench.

As if feeling eyes on him, the pear-shaped man in the checkered suit swung the light through the warehouse. Tabitha was afraid he had heard her growl but he seemed satisfied with his quick sweep with the flashlight and continued on. The sound of keys jangling was clear as he fiddled with the front door lock and let himself out. Once again keys jangled as he secured the door.

Glad he was gone, Tabitha let out her pent-up breath. That sealed her decision. She would investigate the warehouse thoroughly. She aimed for a shiny, lacquered ormolu decorated bookcase, hoping it would soften the jump, and leapt. To her advantage the wood had not been polished in a long while so she hardly slid in the accumulated dust and was able to nimbly jump the rest of the way down to the cement floor inside the warehouse.

Figuring her feline form would be the safest way to look around in case someone else were to appear, Tabitha made her way through the warehouse under and over furniture heading in the direction of the doorway through which the reeky cigar man had passed. Obviously, this part of the warehouse held no secrets so she cut through under a black and gilt Chinese coromandel cabinet, moving quickly, as she wanted to be done before daylight and possible foot traffic through the warehouse.

Without warning and before she could jump back, she heard a snap and sharp blinding pain coursed through her paw, like fire spreading fiercely through her leg. Tabitha yowled like a banshee and the sound echoed through the warehouse eerily. Damn, a mousetrap was firmly clamped on her paw! And there was no way to get it off without shifting into human form. Tabitha tried to wait to see if anyone had heard her pitiful cries of pain, but the warehouse must be truly empty as no one came from the back room.

Tabitha could wait no longer. She shifted as tears coursed down her cheeks onto the hard floor. She had no choice but to sit naked on the cold cement and wait out the pain. Her hand hurt so badly. It was growing a little numb but even that respite was denied as she pried the mousetrap loose and the blood recirculated hotly and caused her to grimace. A thin trickle of blood ran from under the cuticle of two of her fingers. Tabitha resisted the urge to lick the wounds. Man, that smarted beyond mere pain!

Now she was cold and miserable. She looked about for something to wrap about her to keep from freezing. On the wall was an exquisite Aubusson tapestry in blue and green silk, shot with vibrant reds and yellows. Not particular, Tabitha yanked this down and wrapped it about herself. If not warm, it would at least keep the chill off her body. Her fingers stung like the devil but the pain was growing passably bearable and she would be able to continue her investigation. Since no one had come when she had cried out cat-fashion, there must not be anyone else around. But what had the pear-shaped cheap suit been doing in the back room? That Tabitha was determined to find out.

But when she approached the back of the warehouse where she swore he'd come through a door; there was no door. Just a plain cement back wall and a nicely decorated side wall. But no opening of any sort. The side wall was tastefully decorated with a few paintings in gilded frames hanging on display between a pair of Burmese hardwood chiffoniers. Tabitha frowned. Unless the man was a magician, he could not have come from thin air. The wall looked to be simple plaster over drywall. Tabitha ran her hand over it, careful not to bump the paintings.

On closer examination her eyes caught what had been an optical illusion. The paintings weren't real. They were *trompe l'oeil*. Murals painted directly on the wall made to look like framed masterpieces. But wait, so were the chiffoniers! They were all painted onto the wall with great skill and at first glance fooled even Tabitha's discerning scrutiny. Even now, as she looked at them with a jaundiced eye, it was hard to tell, unless you looked sideways and saw they weren't three-dimensional. Just what else wasn't real?

Tabitha ran her fingers over the wall, skimming the surface. The chiffoniers were identical, with decorative rosettes painted on their legs. The one on the left was slightly elliptical. Tabitha pressed the bump and heard a low whirring noise and the wall beneath her fingers began to move, sliding aside, until a generous-sized opening was revealed. A safety light came on briefly then winked out. Someone had gone to a lot of trouble to conceal whatever was behind the wall!

Cautiously Tabitha approached the open chasm and peered inside. It was just an empty warehouse with some large machinery set up and some boxes and crates stacked within. What was the big mystery? Tabitha entered the cavernous room and crept up to one of the machines. It wasn't running and stood like an alien monster, bulky metal and plastic, with rollers, slots and levers, sticking out from the sides. She touched one of the several black rubber rollers with her uninjured hand and drew back as if burned. Something gooey was on her fingers. Oil maybe. Tabitha peered at her fingers in the gloom. It looked like an ink pen had exploded!

Tabitha hated the feel of something on her paws or fingers and was dying to wash it off. She looked about for some paper or rags but there was nothing. The costly Aubusson tapestry Tabitha wore wrapped around her was going to pay the price of this folly. Not completely heartless, Tabitha wiped her hand on the backside of it where matting had been added to bolster the delicate threads.

There were two other monstrous machines in the warehouse. Tabitha ignored these and examined the crates and boxes. One crate was open and next to this stood a box lined with Styrofoam pieces to protect the contents. The crate contained Mexican pottery and clay statues. It appeared these were being repacked into the boxes.

Tabitha opened another crate and found Grecian urns and figurines of nymphs and reproductions of cherubic angels molded in porcelain and resin. Yet another had Chinese dragons and representations of Buddha. These crates were fresh from the harbor and were marked as coming from Mexico, Greece and Hong Kong.

Why in the world would a company order cheap reproductions then immediately repack them and ship them out again? Tabitha checked the various cardboard boxes already taped and ready to send out. They were labeled for Mexico, Greece and Hong Kong. The company obviously wasn't receiving stolen artifacts or shipping them. These cheap gewgaws were of little worth so why bother?

Perplexed Tabitha searched the warehouse for an answer. It had to be here somewhere. The first wave hit her like nausea and she doubled over. Her hands began to tingle and she knew somehow she had touched something in the warehouse Brenton had touched…and recently. She sniffed her fingers and the familiar spicy odor of Tuscany cologne mixed with ink teased her nostrils. The nausea passed and Tabitha straightened up. Perspiration broke out and ran between her breasts. Her body jerked like an electric current was coursing through it at ninety miles an hour and her breath came in panting gasps.

Like an animal hunting its prey Tabitha looked about the warehouse wildly, her eyes seeking every corner, every nook and cranny, almost desperately willing Brenton to step out of the shadows. Up high in the far reaches of the back of the building a thin line of light streaked the air running vertically and horizontally. Tabitha's eyes darted downward to where a rickety wooden staircase ascending to the line of light. There was a door up there!

She scrabbled barefoot against the cement floor trying to get traction as she bolted for the stairway. The heat in her body was so intense Tabitha wondered if instantaneous combustion was a possibility. In the dark she slipped and hit her shin on the badly crafted stairs. Impervious to the pain in her leg or smashed fingers she hoisted herself to her feet and kept on climbing. The stairs seemed to ascend forever until finally, with gasping breath, Tabitha reached the door and twisted the knob. It turned easily, which wasn't a concern, as Tabitha figured to bust it down if it were locked.

The door swung open as she recklessly crashed her shoulder into it, not caring how she found Brenton. She no longer cared if he killed her, but he'd better fuck her first or things were going to get ugly! A yowl built in Tabitha's throat as the oils on the doorknob where Brenton had obviously touched soaked into her pores and brought on a new onslaught of a yearning so deep and primitive she couldn't help but shift into feline form and drop down on all fours.

The Aubusson tapestry tumbled onto the floor of what was a bare-bones office of some sort. The vivid splash of red and blue, green and yellow, against the cheap indoor/outdoor green carpet diverted the figure standing next to a table for a brief moment. The gun in his hand wavered as he caught sight of what seemed to be a red tabby cat in the doorway. But when he blinked and adjusted his eyes it was to find a familiar petite plump figure crouched on all fours. Naked.

"Tabitha? What the hell!"

Tabitha looked up and knew her green eyes were glowing molten like some she-devil possessed by demons, by the way Brenton backed up a step, seeming unsure if he was seeing right or his eyes were playing tricks.

From her vantage point Tabitha saw a surprised Brenton looking unsure and momentarily confused. It was the first time she'd ever seen this expression on his face and that fact alone kept her from jumping on him. She tilted her head in contemplation as her feline instincts battled with her human ones.

Tabitha stayed on all fours and crept forward towards Brenton slowly as if sizing up her prey before pouncing. A slide of thick liquid oozed from her cunt and ran down the inside of her thigh. A sound somewhere between a sigh and a growl emitted from her throat. The sweet acrid smell of her juices floated upward and wafted in the air.

Brenton's eyes visibly clouded as the tangy scent reached his nostrils. Every muscle in his body tensed in a struggle with his common sense. He seemed to be fighting inner demons as his head whipped from side to side, in battle with urges raging within and the gun fell to the table unheeded.

Tabitha rose to her knees and caressed her own breasts, almost savagely tweaking her nipples and uttering mewling cries. "Come to me, Brenton. Don't fight it. Come to me and mount me like the animal within you commands you to. Now! I want you inside me…all the way. Look, this is yours, all yours!" Tabitha reached and parted her labia where the glistening pink lips winked and swelled. She rubbed her clit invitingly, showing Brenton her inner core; the squelching noise of her juices undulated across the room to where Brenton stood, his jaw locked, and sweat beading on his forehead.

All at once he launched himself at her. Tabitha had a momentary breakthrough of sanity and turned around, scrabbling on her knees, seeking escape. The manly smell of Brenton assailed her senses, at the same time his body slammed into hers. The interaction was instantaneous and a voice Tabitha barely recognized as her own shouted, "Fuck me! Please, fuck me!"

Tabitha heard the sound of a belt being jerked off, then a zipper being undone. The engorged cock slid between her butt cheeks but it missed its target in its desperate attempt at coupling. Tabitha nearly screamed in frustration and lowered herself on her elbows, thrusting her ass in the air. "Do it to me now! Brenton, please!"

Whether he understood her cries in his sexual mania or instinct took over, the cock reared back and came on with more adept aim. The thick, hooded head pulsed against the lips of her pussy as it sought entrance. Despite the lubricating liquid that had generously flowed earlier, the ridge of the head lodged for a moment against her opening. Tabitha rocked back and was rewarded with the feeling of being stretched and massaged as the phallus disappeared within and burrowed deep. Her vaginal muscles clenched and released as with every sensation she died a little death of minute unfulfilling orgasms that caused her to shake and tremble. Brenton wedged himself deeper and surged forward biting her on the back of her shoulder as he lunged fully against her. He withdrew a few inches and plunged forward, his balls slapping against her ass in sexual rhythm.

"Give it to me harder!" Tabitha screamed as Brenton drew back and gave it to her again. This time he almost withdrew completely before grasping her around the waist and bringing them together in a humping motion that ground him into her pelvis. He repeated this motion, over and over, until sweat dripped off their bodies and the sound of her juices and his cock straining inside her was all-consuming.

They gasped and grunted as Tabitha found herself being scooted across the floor with each of Brenton's powerful lunges. Finally she braced herself against the wall, on her knees and began to shudder to a climax. But just as she thought she was about to peak, the swell fell away, like a perfect wave, just out of reach. Frustrated, she wanted to grab hold of Brenton and demand he bring her to completion…but he was totally oblivious and strained against her, pumping furiously but not coming.

Tabitha thought if there was a hell, she had put herself and Brenton in it. The craving of wanting to be fucked constantly but not being able to achieve orgasm had to be one of the worst feelings she had ever experienced! She started to beg Brenton to stop. The sound of his balls slapping her ass was sending her near the edge but she knew that was all it would do. The potion only claimed lust for each other, it did not promise fulfillment. But Brenton was helpless to halt his actions and drilled into her over and over.

Tabitha tried to think as the cock plunging into her drove her to distraction. The head and sides of the phallus tunneled and slid, squelching inside her incessantly, until she wanted to scream. How could something so pleasurable bring such agony? They could go mad and fuck themselves to death, mindlessly over and over, heedless of anything else. Suddenly as Brenton hit her womb with a particularly deep stroke and she cried out, the answer came to her. She might not be able achieve an orgasm but she could make Brenton reach his!

As Brenton's rasping breath sounded in her ear, Tabitha cautiously balanced herself against the wall, making certain she could still withstand Brenton's thrusts without falling on her face. She reached behind her to where Brenton's thighs were locked against the back of hers and wedged her small hand between them, burrowing it until she came in contact with Brenton's sacs. They were full of unspent seed and apparently very sensitized from the vigorous unrelieved lovemaking, because when Tabitha enfolded them in her palm and squeezed, Brenton trembled against her.

Tabitha massaged them in the flat of her hand before closing her fingers over their hard contours and milking them with three fingers. Brenton groaned with every motion but kept servicing her, his cock still fully engorged and stiff, working like a piston inside her. Tabitha tried to concentrate on her fingers but every stroke Brenton delivered made her thoughts reel and shy away from her task. Suddenly her fingers unsheathed claws. Her concentration had worked! With renewed vigor Tabitha massaged Brenton's sacs, using the claws to rake over the tender skin as she milked him. Brenton began to tremble and buck into her like a wild animal, but Tabitha kept up the massaging, combined with kneading, using her claws masterfully.

Without further warning Brenton uttered a guttural cry and began to come, his hot semen jetting inside Tabitha like a geyser. To her own astonishment Tabitha's own orgasm spiraled forth as Brenton pumped furiously, as if sensing Tabitha needed his efforts renewed. Tabitha withdrew her hand from Brenton's sacs, as she required both arms to balance as she began to quake and shiver deliciously. Brenton grabbed her hips and undulated against her, groping for her clit with his finger and rubbing it in time with his strokes. Tabitha screamed as her juices released and mingled with Brenton's and she tumbled into an orgasm so strong she may have blacked out, Brenton's cries echoing in her ears as he came again and they both collapsed on the floor.

Chapter Seven

It seemed like hours before either moved, though it must have only been a few minutes as Tabitha came to her senses with Brenton lying on top of her, crushing the breath from her body. She struggled wildly in panic and Brenton shifted his weight. Tabitha gasped as his cock was still wedged inside her and nudged its way out. As it left her, she wasn't sure if she should be relieved or bereft. Her claws were once again sheathed into normal fingernails, confirming she was once again in control...for now.

But it was Brenton's voice, husky and questioning, that brought her to her senses with the same effect as cold water. "Tabitha? What the hell just happened?"

Tabitha wasn't about to go into details about how she had slipped him an overdose of a sexual Mickey and they would be rutting like pigs every five minutes or so unless they visited her grandmother for an antidote. In her mind, first priority was finding out why he had tried to kill her outside O'Malley's and what were his ties to the reeking cigar smoker and this warehouse and...

Ignoring Brenton for a moment, Tabitha sat up, her eyes diverted to the table where moments before Brenton had been standing. Piled neatly in tall stacks was money, gobs of it. Twenties, fifties and hundreds, bundled and sorted.

Brenton's voice came from beside her. "It's not what it looks like. I...you shouldn't have come here and God, you were incredible! And..."

Tabitha looked at the money then looked at Brenton, her eyes narrowing. "And you tried to kill me! Damn you, you lured me to O'Malley's then tried to run me down all for this? What the hell did I do to you, Brenton Calder?"

"You took nine thousand dollars that was in Diamond Charlie's possession." Brenton seemed to be coming out of his daze, and realizing his pants and briefs were around his ankles over his Ferragamo loafers, he got to his feet, kicking off the shoes in an attempt to straighten his shirt and pants.

"My life is only worth nine freakin' thousand dollars?" Tabitha was spitting mad.

"You don't understand. And I didn't try to kill you. I..."

Tabitha saw the clouded look coming into Brenton's eyes and scrambled to her feet. They were the darkest of blue, like a stormy ocean before a hurricane. She had to get away from him before... Brenton had pulled at his pants to straighten the creases. He was between her and the door when Tabitha smelled the musky scent emanating from both the man and his clothes. Tabitha swore her bones were melting and her hands clenched and unclenched as Brenton kicked off his pants and briefs and strode towards her. His confusion of moments earlier was gone, as he knew his purpose now. It was one thing and one thing only as he drew closer and knelt before her.

His hands with their long tapered fingers reached up and nudged her legs apart. Tabitha obliged by assuming an open stance. His face was only inches from her slit as he inhaled her fragrance. The hands grasp her butt cheeks and held tight as he brought his mouth to her cunt and ran his tongue over her labia thrusting it inside her without a word and suckling at her juices. The flicking motion against her textured walls made Tabitha gasp and quake. Her knees rode up and down, her body undulating against Brenton's tongue and face. He encouraged her motions as his hands on her ass drew her back and forth.

The wave came, threatening to crash as her clit was teased and her juices coaxed forth with a sudden gush. But just as before the wave ebbed, then spiraled with twice the force, but not to break and let Tabitha have her release. She realized whatever drastic magic the potion worked, her own orgasm depended on Brenton's. They were linked in more ways than one.

Her head thrashed back and forth in frustration as Brenton sucked as if to drain her. She couldn't take much more of this as she grabbed Brenton's thick sandy hair and pulled his head up from her musky depths. Desperately, she breathed hoarsely, "You have to fuck me now or I'll go crazy. Do you understand? I can't come unless you come! Ohhh!" This was caused as Brenton took his long middle finger and shoved it inside her working it in and out against her clit and deep within.

"Oh, I understand." His voice sounded assured, "You've given me some sort of drug, Tabitha Fenwick. What was it, some sort of derivative of Spanish Fly or Goat Weed? It doesn't matter because, yes, I'll fuck you and I'll fuck you so hard and so deep you'll scream for me to stop, then beg for me to continue. But I'll fuck you when I'm good and ready and not before. Got it?" He shoved another finger inside her, causing Tabitha to writhe up and down pantomiming copulation with his hand. The hand working her masterfully pulled away from her pussy and Brenton stood before her, holding his fingers out to her. "Do you want me to fuck you? Do you?"

His rigid cock prodded against her stomach, drawing Tabitha's eyes hungrily. "Yes! Damn you! Yes!"

"Then suck my fingers. Taste yourself on them. Taste and swallow. That's a girl."

Tabitha took his fingers between her lips and sampled her own musky sweet and sour juices. Sucking gently almost cautiously.

"Harder," Brenton demanded.

Tabitha took his fingers into her mouth and sucked at them, tasting more of her own coating, cleaning the digits with her tongue. Brenton was nudging her legs and Tabitha moved her feet further apart but he kept pushing against her until she backed up and her butt wedged against the table where the money was stacked.

With a sudden savage movement Brenton knocked the stacks over creating a bed of money. He pulled his fingers from Tabitha's mouth and grabbed her hips lifting her on top of the money heap. Tabitha tried to bring him to her wet, moist center but Brenton merely laughed and ordered, "Draw your legs up under you, then lay back and spread your thighs. I want to see my cock moving in and out of you, doing to you what you've managed to do to me with this drug you slipped me. Do it!"

Hungrily Tabitha complied. Luckily her limbs were pliable and adept at stretching. Even so when she lay back and displayed herself wide open, she gasped as the big head of Brenton's cock nudged against her nether lips and forged inside. He took his time, only giving her a little and taking it back. Tabitha watched his face as he watched her and his cock moving at his command.

"Will you beg now, sweet Tabitha? Or in a moment?" To punctuate this he moved forward and teased that he was going to plunge all the way in but he stepped back and only the opening of her cunt was rewarded with his girth.

Tabitha caught her breath then let it out in frustration while he played with her emotions.

"Look up, Tabitha. See me *almost* fucking you. Mocking you with my power."

Tabitha looked up at the ceiling where the fluorescent panels had glare guards to protect against the light reflection. But the panels also reflected the struggle below as Tabitha watched Brenton's cock partway inside her. Moving, but not penetrating her depths. The sight made her blood surge with want. "Go deeper, Brenton! Deeper!"

"Like this?"

Tabitha saw an inch more disappear as it scraped against her walls, teasing her into thinking it was more. Her cunt contracted as it was fooled by the simulation and released its cream. She shuddered and tried to ignore her craving but it was ravenous!

"You like that, don't you? I feel your juices anointing the tip of my cock and I want you to feel me slam into you all the way to the hilt. We both can come and be done with this nonsense. All you have to do is tell me what you gave me, Tabitha. What hellish drug did you slip me to make me crave your sweet pussy like fine wine?"

Tabitha's voice was a half-groan, half-plea, "I can't tell you what..." His cock began pulling out. "No! It's an old herbal remedy. I swear. We have to go to get the antidote. Please!"

His pulsing cock halted. "You mean this is not something that wears off?"

"I..." Tabitha took the opportunity and his uncertainty to unfold her legs and bring them against the back of Brenton's thighs, flinging him forward. His cock burrowed deep and Tabitha bucked against him, riding him hard.

Brenton lost his edge as undeniably his balls tightened and his cock expanded to further engorged girth as it was teased and milked. He spiraled towards release but his orgasm did not come and he cried out as the blood pooled in the tip of his penis causing it to swell painfully.

Tabitha was relentless in her pursuit and sensed his discomfort in his bunched muscles throughout his back and shoulders. "You must come for me to come and vice versa. I can make your cock swell without release just as you torture me. So what say we stop this silliness and work together until we get the antidote or it's going to be a painful rough road?"

Brenton cried out as she ground against his swollen flesh. "All right. But you have some explaining to do. Jeez!"

Tabitha forced him deep to shut him up. Her family secrets were not about to become public knowledge. Besides, Brenton had the explaining to do. The money underneath her was proof enough of that! She unlocked her legs and reached for Brenton's testicles. "Move with me as I stroke your balls, Brenton. That'll bring you release. And you must bring mine at the same time. Suck my tits and..."

"I know how to make a woman come!" Brenton growled.

Tabitha narrowed her eyes. Why had she fallen for such a jerk! She grabbed his sacs with more gusto than she intended and Brenton responded by clamping his teeth down on one of her nipples, so hard she arched forward. Brenton relinquished his bite and laved the areola with his tongue, flicking it back and forth.

Tabitha returned the favor by massaging his balls and pressing firmly between them, lifting them and cradling them in her palm as her thumb manipulated them.

The blood in Brenton's cock circulated and the ache dulled as he moved in and out with a rhythmic cadence that brought Tabitha's hips up to meet his. His lips on her breast licked and sucked, but as Tabitha stroked him below he began to groan and tremble. Suddenly he shot his load deep inside her, bucking forward and holding her still as he plunged in and out, taking his pleasure and ignoring hers.

But though he came, the initial orgasm did not reach a crescendo and instead he merely quaked in the throes of a never-ending torture. He was coming over and over but he could not stop! His essence was spilled time and time again as it was pumped from him but there was no finale. "Oh, my god! Ahhh! Do something, you witch!"

"I'm not a witch! I'm a…never mind. I have to come or you won't have any peace. That seems to be the ground rules." Tabitha tried to disengage from him but he was locked inside her, still rocked by sensations he could not stop. She was forced to guide his hand to her clit and keep it there by covering it with her own and guiding him in the motions of teasing her, stroking her, all the while his cock buried deep inside her, pulsing repeatedly. "That's it. Good. Ahhh, I feel it coming. Rub faster, Brenton. Faster!" Suddenly she erupted in a primal scream as she quivered beneath him.

At the same moment Brenton let out a cry of both relief and total lust as he crested and his muscles went lax, trembling from the extreme exertion. Finally it was over! He pulled out of Tabitha and stepped to the side, needing the table to support his weight. "I swear I don't want sex again for at least six months."

Tabitha lowered her legs and looked about at the money they had christened with sex. She tried to clean off the rivulets of Brenton's jism, mingled with her own juices that were running down the inside of her thighs. "From the way this has been working, I'd say you have about six minutes give or take before you prove yourself wrong on that score."

"What the hell did you do to me?" Brenton swore. "We have to get away from each other."

"I think it's too late for that. Once we consummate it's all we'll think about between cycles. If I remember the warning, we'll probably die trying to get to each other or…"

"You're joking right?"

"Does your eternal orgasm seem like a joke?"

"Fuck! What do we do now?"

"That's what we're going to do until we get to my grandmother's for the cure."

"You owe me an explanation for this, big-time. And then you're fired!"

Brenton looked incredibly sexy in just his shirt, Tabitha thought, even if he had just fired her. Wait a minute, it was too soon for another sex cycle. Eww, she was still attracted to him, jerk and hit-and-run killer aside. "You go first, Brenton. We'll talk while we get going. Hop to it or we won't get far before another fuckfest."

He looked at her as though she'd just popped a cork. But what could she do but remain practical? She watched him step into his pants and grab his shoes.

"Where are your clothes?" He looked her over appreciatively despite the fact they'd already had torrid sex twice.

"Uh, outside. Don't ask... It's a long story and you wouldn't believe it."

"I don't think I want to know. Here put on my shirt. You must be freezing."

"I'm not going to have much chance of that. Let's go." But she donned his shirt gratefully.

He looked at the mounds of money, uneasily. "This will have to wait. And you have to give back that nine thousand."

"That's severance pay."

"The hell it is. It's blood money. Diamond Charlie's and yours if you don't return it."

They were through the door and at the top of the rickety staircase. "Are you threatening me again, Brenton?"

"I never threatened you."

"What about the car in front of O'Malley's?"

"Look, Tabitha, I was aiming for that guy behind you. He was going to—"

"Yeah, the same guy I saw leaving here tonight. I smell a rat, Brenton, and—"

"And I smell your sweet cunt juices. Come here."

Tabitha had lost track of time, as they were halfway down the stairs. "Brenton, we can't..."

But the words were no sooner out than Brenton's lips were on hers and she smelled sex, her sex on him, all over him. She opened her mouth and encouraged his tongue to explore. His hands were on the hemline of the shirt she wore, raising it slightly to caress her bareness, sliding a finger inside her and flicking her clit maddeningly. The feel of his jism drying on her thighs seemed to make him hornier, like he was turned on by the marking of his territory. The finger withdrew as his pants were undone and his hardness entered her without a word. They both seemed in mutual agreement if they were going to get anywhere they needed to be attuned to each other's needs and what got them off.

Tabitha simply locked her legs around him, using the stair railing to brace her back, hoping it would hold. She always landed on her feet but Brenton would receive the shock of his life if the woman he'd been making love to suddenly grew a tail after falling ten feet.

Brenton reached behind her as he quickened his lunges and stroked her rump. Tabitha thought nothing of it until a pressure at her anus made her groan deep in her throat just as something penetrated her. She nearly came undone as the sensitive tissue was manipulated and stretched. Whatever it was felt wonderful as it stroked against her in conflict with the cock moving in and out of her cunt. She realized Brenton was going to have to come too or she would never reach completion.

But Brenton seemed to be having no trouble as he withdrew and plunged, peaking quickly. His orgasm rocketed, just as did Tabitha's and they collapsed against each other, trying to regain their strength quickly. Brenton pulled his cock and the object from her anus out simultaneously and Tabitha trembled at the start of another orgasm that had nothing to do with the spell.

Brenton held her tightly against him. "Why the hell did you do something so crazy? I wanted you, Tabitha, but it was too dangerous. It was for your own good that I didn't...that we didn't hook up. You don't know what you've done." He held her away and looked into her face, his eyes clear and totally cognizant. "Damn!" he swore under his breath. He tossed something over the railing, before hiking up his pants and grabbing her wrist. "Let's go."

They were down the stairs and at the open sliding panel when Tabitha asked, "What was that?"

"What?" He pushed the button in the painted on chiffonier and the panel slid shut as if it was just a stationary wall.

"That thing you put inside me."

"Did you like it?" He looked at her curiously.

"Maybe."

"It was a glow wand." He laughed; surprised he still had a sense of humor after the recent events.

"You're kidding? One of those things kids use at Halloween?" Tabitha sounded incredulous as they made their way around furniture in the darkened Oriental Dragon warehouse.

"And strippers use them to... Well, you know, they shove them like that and in the front, to mesmerize their customers."

"No, I didn't know. But what were you doing with it?"

"I have a couple of them to dot the corner of the money to mark it for identification purposes." Brenton sounded uneasy as if he didn't want to further comment.

"Look, Brenton, you are going to tell me what's going on or…"

"Or what?" He reached in his pocket and took out a key. The front door was unlocked and relocked on the outside as they passed through and stood on Cobble Street.

"Or maybe I don't take you to where the cure is and we fuck like bunnies until we perish."

"Intriguing idea and now that I know what turns you on it's not so bad." Brenton sounded genuinely amused. "As a matter of fact, I can't think of any other way I'd like to go out of this world. Being buried deep in you is a dream come true. But you seem to have turned it into a nightmarish twist with this sexual drug. What were you thinking?"

Tabitha had the grace to blush. "I… Wait a minute. How did you come without my help just now?"

Brenton sounded surprised. "I don't know. I felt you and… I don't know how to explain it. I mean I felt you from within, your body became my body and…" He stopped mid-sentence. "This is stupid. What have you got me believing? Cures. Antidotes to a sex potion. Look, I think you've brainwashed me into believing something impossible. Get your clothes and go back to the hotel. Wait for me there. I'll come when…if I can."

"Brenton, you don't understand. We can't be separated or…"

"Or what? We'll howl at the moon and go crazy with lust? Tell me another tall tale." He walked away from her;

probably meaning to walk around the block until she was gone then he'd go back into the warehouse.

Tabitha was powerless to stop him. He had to find out for himself. She walked around to the side where her clothes lay in a heap. She no longer needed the overalls and it was a waste of time to wear pants so she carried the items with her back down the alley into the abandoned fish market and onto Old Harbor Road. Heat radiated through her breasts and down into her groin, tiny pulses shooting through her cunt. The call of the potion was beckoning.

The Vanquish was still parked in the alley, minus its aluminum alloy wheel covers. Tabitha thought it was a generous case of light vandalism under the circumstances and started to get in the car. Without warning she was grabbed from behind and propelled back, then pivoted against the elegantly sloped hood. Brenton's harsh voice grated in her ears.

"Do you want to know how I found you? I tracked you. I smelled you like a dog sniffs out a bitch in heat! What have you done to me?"

"Brenton, I told you..."

But the words were torn from her as he grabbed her legs and threw them around his waist. His pants were unzipped and his erect cock reared outward and towards her. It found entrance at once and plunged all the way to the hilt, driving the breath from Tabitha with its force. It rocked inside her, causing shooting sparks to spiral in waves as she cried out for release.

Brenton showed no mercy as he worked her cunt fiercely, making Tabitha pay for what she'd done. Tabitha had little choice but to take what Brenton dished out. She didn't understand everything that was happening with the potion but it seemed to depend on her and Brenton cooperating as one to achieve release. Each time one of them had resisted, neither could achieve orgasm without the other. Just as she suspected Brenton was building to a crescendo of feverish thrusting, but it was fruitless. "Brenton, listen to me."

"Now is not the time." He grunted as he shoved his cock deeper trying to get off.

"You don't understand." A particularly deep thrust made Tabitha gasp. If she couldn't make him understand they were both going to either die of exhaustion or be so sore they would scream in pain as they copulated incessantly. "Brenton, don't resist the pull of desire. We both have to get off at the same time, but only if you don't fight the impulse. Ahhh, right there." She groaned as a shiver raced through her but the approaching orgasm wouldn't let her go. "On the stairs, you were able to come separately but you weren't fighting it. Don't fight now! Do you hear me? Let it come. Relax."

She could only hope she got through to him as he shifted her on the hood and grabbed her butt and pulled her against him rubbing her clit as he shoved her back and forth. Tabitha resolved to take her own advice and concentrated on relaxing, savoring the cock pulsing within her as part of herself, not an intruder that had forced its way inside her. She imagined herself riding a horse bareback, up and down in a graceful cadence. A ripple undulated and whorled through her body as her clit was rubbed faster and a rush of juice let loose and coated the hard staff servicing her. It felt right, for Brenton to be her master and mount her like an animal. For what were they but two animals rutting in the early morning light?

"Yes, that's it, Brenton. Give it to me!" No sooner did she acquiesce to the feeling of being subdued by this human than she peaked and called his name huskily as she tumbled over the falls and her orgasm washed over her like a flow of hot lava.

Attuned to Tabitha's release Brenton came with a gush, pumping his hot seed deep within her as he cried out and collapsed heavily against her with a moan that was half-sob, half-curse. "You've bewitched me. I don't know how, but you have."

"Shhh. Brenton, you have to give in." Tabitha tried to move but he had her legs still wrapped around him. "Don't you see? Every time we fight it, we can't get satisfaction and we are driven to keep going until we make each other come in sync."

He pulled out of her wetness, standing on shaky legs as she continued. "Next time, go with it and it won't be so difficult. You have to feel what I feel and I have to be in tune with you."

"Next time? I don't think I can. I want you, Tabitha, potion or not, but right now there is no way in hell I can do it again anytime soon."

"You can and will. But remember to go with it and I promise it will be good, very good. It doesn't seem to be just about sex but something more."

Brenton appeared to just become aware of his immediate surroundings and the fact they had had sex in an alley. He zipped his pants and walked a few paces away, looking in disbelief. "What is my car doing here?"

"Come on, Brenton. There's no time for that. We have to get to Victorian Hill as fast as we can. You'll have to drive."

"Damned right. It's my car and…what the hell happened to the wheel covers? They're gone! Son of a…"

"Brenton, please! Just get in and drive, but be careful. I don't know how far…and when we…well, with you driving there may be room for sex in the driver's seat and I know it will be at least thirty minutes before we reach Grandmother's." Tabitha's voice was matter of fact as she climbed into the passenger seat and handed Brenton the keys as he got in. She even started to fasten the seat belt until she realized how risky that was going to be in a matter of minutes.

To Brenton's credit, he remained quiet, except for a few mumbles about his vandalized car. Tabitha was glad as they drove away from the dock area and crossed the first busy intersection. She began to feel hot and cold then a searing flash of heat pierced deep inside her cunt. "No! Not here. Not now," she groaned.

Brenton glanced over to her and saw her scooting down in the passenger seat. The shirt she wore bunched up her thighs and in the early light her burgundy bush was clearly visible. "God, you have the most beautiful pussy I've ever seen!"

Any other time Tabitha would have gotten a chuckle over his choice of phrasing but right now all she wanted was to feel his tongue in her beautiful bush, parting her labia and sucking her until she creamed. She pushed her small hands down and rubbed her mound, sliding a finger over the lips, then parting them.

"Let me watch you," Brenton breathed huskily, one eye on the road. His head constantly turning to peruse Tabitha's movements.

Tabitha turned sideways, using the car door to brace her back. She parted her pink cunt lips and showed Brenton the inside where moisture was bringing a pearly sheen to the outer rim. "Is this what you want?" she purred softly, running her finger over herself, moving her clit back and forth.

"Yeah," he breathed. "Put your finger inside and fuck yourself, slowly...very slowly."

Tabitha inserted her index finger inside herself and moved it back and forth. Her finger was small and not doing it for her so she inserted her middle finger.

"Slower, babe." Brenton growled. "Open your legs more and hold yourself open so I can see. That's it."

Tabitha squirmed in her seat but her fingers were unfulfilling after what she'd already been through. She sighed restlessly then noticed Brenton had unzipped his pants and had a massive hard-on. It was to be expected after all.

"Move over here, Tabitha. Let me feel you."

Tabitha scooted across the seat, keeping her back to the door. Her legs were still open, the left crooked to fit on the seat and the right dangling over. She placed herself next to Brenton in the same prone position.

Brenton kept one hand on the wheel and the right one splayed over Tabitha's mound, his thumb flicking her clit. Without warning he thrust his index and middle finger inside her and worked them furiously. Remembering what she had to do, Tabitha forced herself to relax and go with the sensations. The fingers were long and reached deep, touching her textured walls, his thumb grazing her clit repeatedly. Back and forth, his fingers fucking her. It felt good, sooo good. Tabitha reared up as her orgasm ripped through her with the force of a rocket. She cried and clenched against the fingers deep within her, holding them until she stopped trembling.

Brenton watched her from beneath hooded lids as he drove. He had been forced to slow down as he watched Tabitha come and now as he withdrew his fingers he brought them up to his nose and mouth, inhaling her fragrance.

Tabitha noticed his hard-on was painfully swollen and had to be killing him but he breathed not a word to indicate his agony. She reached over and touched the hood of his cock, then lying flat on her stomach stretching out across the seat, she placed her lips against the tip.

They drove over a dip in the road causing the ramrod stiff cock to push into her mouth. Brenton caught his breath. And Tabitha took the cue, bobbing up and down on the phallus, coaxing it to circulate the blood and give Brenton pleasure and not pain. She let the swollen staff touch the back of her throat as she closed her throat muscles over it and sucked gently then harder.

Brenton's hips of their own volition moved up and down, enticingly suggestive. He flipped the switch and moved the steering column up out of the way as Tabitha began sucking in earnest, caressing with suction and manipulating his balls with her small soft hands. Brenton let out a guttural growl and shot his load, the jism hitting Tabitha's throat and sliding down the passage like a sexual sundae, slow and hot. She milked him as long as she could and when she raised her head, it was to find Brenton had pulled the car over and closed his eyes.

"Are you okay?" she asked, looking up from his lap.

"Oh, yeah," he muttered softly, stroking the back of her hair. "Come here."

Tabitha knew the potion spell was not on them at that moment. She knew the tingling sensation it elicited and the hot and cold differential it caused. Now it was just her and Brenton. She raised herself up and looked eye to eye with the man who confused the hell out of her. She didn't know what he was into. She didn't know what he was going to do to her in the future. Right now was the only thing important. The only thing that mattered.

His hand on the back of her neck pushed her towards him. His lips locked over hers and she melted into his body. His tongue licked the inside of her mouth, tasting his own come, and the smell of Tabitha's juices pervaded his senses. Tabitha knew this, as she tasted what he tasted and smelled what he smelled. It was intoxicating, absolutely delicious!

They kissed for what seemed an eternity until each came to the same realization at the same time. They weren't raging hot for each other like two love-starved teenagers. But they were turned on naturally. Brenton stared at her for a moment before pulling the car back on the road. They made it to the older part of town and no sudden lust manias occurred.

Tabitha wasn't sure what this meant and worse she wasn't sure she welcomed it. She missed the closeness with Brenton, natural or unnatural. She recognized the surroundings as they started up the twisting, turning drive to her grandmother's mansion. The morning was gray with wisps of fog floating through the air, especially going up the hill. The cloak of the fog hid the house until they were right on it. Tabitha didn't mean to bark at Brenton but he almost bypassed the driveway. "Turn in here!"

Brenton shot a glance at her before cranking the wheel a hard right. The house looked deserted but Tabitha knew it wasn't and unseen eyes watched their approach.

Before the car had come to a complete stop Tabitha hopped out the door and beckoned to Brenton. "Hurry! Come on!"

Brenton frowned. "I don't care to be ordered about like some lackey."

Tabitha's eyes narrowed before a flash of white-hot need knifed through her stomach and down into her cunt. She gasped and shook her head, fighting the wave of animal lust that made her eyes grow dark and begin to glow. She realized it must have something to do with tension between her and Brenton that caused the lust potion to take effect. Grandmother would know.

The words were out before she could stop them. "Shut up and come into the house with me."

Brenton was by her side in two seconds and propelled her up the steps towards the house. He backed her against the wood siding and groped her breasts through the shirt. "I'm going to fuck you for that!"

Tabitha saw by the glazed look in his eyes the lust was on him, but she couldn't do a damned thing about it, as the hot blood coursed into her vagina. "Then do it! Now!"

His zipper was still down and his cock reared out almost obscenely. Tabitha reached down and moved the tails of her shirt aside and parted her labia, showing Brenton her hole, moist and waiting. He grasped the base of his cock and brought it to her opening, pushing the head in. Tabitha released her cunt lips and they stroked over the hood inviting it to burrow inside.

But Brenton needed no invitation as he plowed forth and deep inside Tabitha. His hands on her ass cheeks raised her up hard against him as he moved her back and forth, listening to her cries as his cock hit her womb then pulled almost out completely before plummeting deep inside again. Tabitha's cries rose, as did Brenton's as she gasped out, "Brenton, we have to agree not to disagree. Remember in the car when we kissed, how that felt. We won't come unless we learn to be in tune…ohhh."

Brenton had shoved her against his pelvis and began small strokes keeping himself deep within her. The spiral began but it refused to crest and Tabitha was left quivering at the beginning of an orgasm that wouldn't come. "Please, Brenton!"

He paused, her cries having reached some part of him still susceptible to compassion. His cock was throbbing inside Tabitha, hard and unforgiving, but Brenton stopped moving and looked deep into Tabitha's green eyes, his blue ones tinged around the irises with wonder. "It's all right Tabitha. It's all right. Let it come. I can feel you wrapped around me. I want you to let me come inside you. That's it, milk me, contract around me. Invite me to fill you with my hot jism. Uhhh!"

A jet of come spurted into her triggering a chain reaction. She cried out and began to quake. Brenton pushed in and out using friction to bring her over the edge as he came again and she welcomed him within her, murmuring in his ear, "Come for me, darling. Just for me and I'll return the favor. Oh, my God!" The incredible swell that overtook them both left them clasping each other feverishly.

Tabitha looked into Brenton's eyes and they were completely clear of the potion's effects. Her own body was languid and heavy causing her to sag against Brenton in blissful relief.

They both came back to their senses with the uncanny feeling they were being watched.

Chapter Eight

Tabitha gasped as her sister looked on with undisguised curiosity written all over her face. "Seline! You shouldn't—"

"I shouldn't? I don't think I'm the one open to censure. So that's what sex looks like? Fascinating, especially when he put that into you and…" Seline rubbed her breasts through her knitted sweater. "I feel all tingly." Her dual-colored eyes shone with an inner glow.

"Seline! You know you can't. The Spellspeak power will diminish if you experience the awakening before you are initiated. Oh my god, Grandmother is going to kill me!" Tabitha pulled at the shirt barely covering her thighs, not just in modesty, but in anxiety over what Seline had witnessed.

Brenton had remained silent until now. "Spellspeak? Power? You are all loony, Tabitha. Your whole family is flipping nuts! I'm getting out of here." Brenton was halfway down the steps of the wraparound porch when a voice like velvet steel rang out from the front doorway.

"Stop! At once!"

As if anchors weighted down his legs, Brenton's gait slowed to a mere shuffle.

The voice commanded. "Come here."

Brenton turned and saw an older woman standing in the front doorway. He was powerless to disobey and climbed back up the porch. Tabitha watched, knowing

Grandmother was using her power to lure Brenton into the house. It was Tabitha's turn next.

"Seline. Tabitha. Come inside." Her grandmother's voice was falsely lilting, sweet with a tinge of arsenic undertones.

When she was inside Tabitha dare not glance to Brenton who stood by the staircase.

Her grandmother's voice demanded full attention. "Seline, what did you see?"

Obediently Seline recounted matter-of-factly; "I saw Tabitha's private parts open for this man's phallus. They joined in great energy but there was no love just lust. Until the end, then I felt the power emanate from them."

Tabitha blushed at what her sister had seen and what her grandmother had heard.

"Enough!" Her grandmother ordered. "How did it make you feel, Seline?"

Seline looked confused. "I felt strange but I don't know. I wanted to feel their passion but I do not know how."

Grandmother lowered her voice soothingly. "'Tis all right, child. In time you will understand. But not yet. Go to your room and cant the Spellspeak Targa and Energa spell until you are calm and no longer burn with the internal heat in your private parts." She waited until Seline was gone up the stairs then turned, her anger rekindled at her other granddaughter. "And you! Did I not warn you about the danger of the potion? You said he wanted you at one time but that is not so, is it?"

Tabitha began, "I—"

"Silence!"

Tabitha's tongue was unable to form words and she knew Brenton was equally impotent. Grandmother's power was strong.

The older woman continued. "You know how I concluded you lied, my child? The potion tells me! The lust rages unchecked when both are not in agreement. It is designed for troubled marriages and relationships to teach symbiotic joining. Each partner must please the other to reach fulfillment. But you two, going at it like alligators, angry, joining only for your own lust. It is wise you have come to me before it grows worse."

Brenton's tongue formed the words, "Worse? How much worse can it get?"

"With the minute amount of the dose I prescribed, not much. You would burn your yen for copulation out in a week."

"A week?" Brenton was dazed, Tabitha judged by the incomplete conversation, but he grasped the main points. "Unadulterated sex every ten minutes for a week? I don't think I can."

"Oh, you will, young man. Believe me. There is no denying the potion unless you both are attuned to each other and stay that way. Then the lust remains at bay."

That explained the drive over when the spell seemed to leave them alone, Tabitha realized. But there was one problem. "Uh, Grandmother. I didn't use the prescribed dose. I doubled and…"

"Child! Did I teach you nothing of caution while you were apprenticed? Do you know what you have done? The danger, the unknown of using a forbidden potion in an unprescribed and reckless manner. Not to mention the years of Seline's teaching you could have endangered and annulled. I am more disappointed in you, child, than I have ever been before." The deep lines furrowing the older woman's brow and the sorrow in her eyes were Tabitha's undoing.

She crumpled at her grandmother's feet, in total disregard to her state of half-undress. "I am sooo sorry, Grandmother. I know you told me and I did not listen. I thought if the potion was weak from age I could double it, but I should have known better. I don't know why I am so bad. I could not be your successor and caused Seline to be deprived of a normal life and now this. Please forgive me, Grandmother, and I will never disobey you. Ever!" Tabitha couldn't help the sobs that racked her.

Hands on her shoulders propelled her to her feet and Tabitha thought it was her beloved grandmother but the fingers were longer and thicker. Brenton drew her against him. "I don't pretend to know what the hell is going on but it'll be all right, Tabitha. Shhh!" He smoothed her hair.

Tabitha's grandmother watched this scene with a wizened look on her face. Perhaps she was wrong about these two. The man came to her granddaughter's aid unbidden, despite her deceit. "I will prepare the antidotal draught. Tabitha, take your man up to the Octagonal chamber and both of you bathe, but remain undressed. I will bring the remedy with further instructions in one hour."

Tabitha seemed to take strength both from Brenton and her grandmother. She pulled away from Brenton and led him up the dark, twisting staircase and down a long, dim hall to one of many closed doors.

Brenton was being very complacent about the most recent events and was taking this new bizarre request in stride. Tabitha realized he must be exhausted from lack of sleep and hyper-sex. Or maybe it was Grandmother's hypnotic power that had hold of him, or a combination of all three. But he came to life as she opened the door to a room whose shape lived up to its name.

The Octagonal chamber was exactly that, with the sole furniture a bed stripped of all covers and only a mattress on a raised dais. The angled walls were painted with symbols that were a mixture of Egyptian, Celtic and Bodiccean. Niches in the walls held candles, which for some inexplicable reason were already lit as if the room knew it would have occupants.

The candlelight flickered across the walls making the symbols shimmer as if they crawled and danced ancient movements. Brenton took one look at this bizarre room and balked. "Uh-uh, Tabitha. I don't know what you did to me and I don't care if your family considers themselves some sort of cult or witchcraft practicing devils worshippers, but I'll be damned if I'm going to be sacrificed!"

Tabitha laid a hand on his arm. "Brenton. It's not like that. Don't get worked up or you know what will happen. We haven't taken the cure yet. The bathroom is through that door. It's quite normal and modern. Go ahead and shower. You'll see it'll all be clearer when you've had some sleep. Which will be soon, I promise."

Brenton entered the Octagonal room cautiously, skirting the bed and the symbol embossed walls. He disappeared into the adjoining bathroom and moments later Tabitha heard the control spigots turn and water spraying from the shower. She gave Brenton space but did not go too far as the potion was bound to have some effect if they were distanced from each other.

When Brenton appeared wrapped in a towel, she was sitting on the edge of the elevated bed, trying to keep her eyes open. "See, the bed is harmless. But quite comfortable. There's a stairway on the side to get up here. Why don't you lie down while I shower? It'll be another half hour before Grandmother comes."

Brenton remained quiet and when Tabitha came out of the bathroom, clean and fresh, her hair washed and hanging wet, he was sitting on the bottom stair of the dais, dozing off. Tabitha smiled at his distrust of lying on the bed. She had wrapped a fluffy towel around herself and felt pretty good, all things considered.

When a discreet knock came at the door, Brenton's eyes flew open and his hand slid down the towel he wore as if searching for something. Tabitha remembered the gun he had been holding at the warehouse. Was he so accustomed to being armed it was second nature when he was startled to reach for his weapon? Just what the hell *was* he into?

Tabitha's grandmother entered carrying an ornate silver tea tray with two glasses that resembled twisted champagne flutes. She whispered a few words to Tabitha but Brenton's voice overrode their conversation. "I want to hear exactly what is being said. I'm a little low on trust at this point."

Grandmother smiled in understanding. "Of course. I was explaining to Tabitha you each must drink this draught at the same time, then lie on the bed. It works quickly but you must lie still for it to erase the effects of the other potion."

Brenton looked at the two glasses on the tray suspiciously. "How do I know this isn't some sort of trick?"

Tabitha sighed. "Brenton, you have to trust me. Besides, what else could happen than what has already?"

"You could poison me. You and your crazy family." Brenton glared, then groaned as his body betrayed him and his cock grew hard.

"Hurry, now!" Tabitha's grandmother coaxed. "Both of you. Get on the bed and drink this."

Tabitha took the glasses from the tray and carried one to Brenton. As soon as she was near him, she shivered. The lust spell was making its presence known. It was feeding on Brenton's tenseness and distrust towards her. Desperately, Tabitha grabbed Brenton's arm and tried to propel him up the dais. It was too late!

Brenton wrenched his arm away from Tabitha's touch as a hot flame shot from her fingers into his body. The delicate glass he held fell to the floor, but did not shatter. Strangely enough it landed upright with nary a drop of liquid spilled.

Tabitha looked towards where her grandmother had stood but she had discreetly gone, knowing her presence was unwanted and awkward. Tabitha's towel was ripped from her body and she lost her grip on her own glass. It too fell, but did not shatter, landing upright as had its mate, still holding the draught.

Brenton grabbed her wrist and twisted her towards him. His towel fell to the floor and his cock stood out rock-hard and angry. Tabitha tried not to inhale his fragrance and scooted to the wall. But Brenton was a beast on the prowl and stalked her, boldly holding his cock in one hand. "It's no use. Breathe me, smell me, so I don't suffer alone. I am going to fuck you, and you know you want it so bad, you'll cry for me."

His eyes were glazed over and Tabitha knew it was no use. She let out her pent-up breath and let the scent of Brenton fill her nostrils. Instantly a flood of syrupy liquid was released from her cunt and she was hot and ready for him. Her back was to the wall when Brenton reached her. She made a last ditch effort to resist by locking her legs together and in that moment she swore the walls were whispering, the symbols and ancient signs shifting beneath her back and butt. Hands that were not Brenton's were on her ankles, spreading them apart, holding her in manacles. Other hands locked around her waist and came from behind to part her nether lips for Brenton's entrance.

Tabitha could not move. It was the ancient curse of the potion seeking retribution for her disrespect. Oh, God! What would happen to her and to Brenton?

But Brenton seemed oblivious to the hands and maybe they were invisible to him. Maybe it was Tabitha's curse alone as the tip of his cock nudged against her splayed vaginal lips. Then hands propelled her forward, impaling her on his stiff shaft. Tabitha caught her breath as fingers manipulated her ass. Hands parted her cheeks and something invaded her from behind. Her anus tried to tighten against the probing but assured fingers massaged her puckered opening until the sphincter relaxed and stretched.

Brenton was too involved in feeling her cunt around his throbbing cock to notice anything else. His hands were on her breasts kneading them into hard mounds that ached to be suckled.

The walls shuddered and whispered ancient ritualistic words in a tongue long forgotten. Tabitha's anus expanded further as she was plundered from behind. It was a penis. She knew the feel of pliable skin versus an inanimate object, but it wasn't Brenton's. This one was different, uncircumcised, the rough edges of the foreskin causing extra friction that made Tabitha squirm.

But the hands held her as Brenton laved her breasts with his tongue, sucking on the areola until it tightened and puckered. His cock began to move in a staccato rhythm that Tabitha could not follow. The phallus in her ass moved in opposite rhythm. Tabitha was a sexual seesaw, fucked front and back. It was heaven and hell all rolled into one, exquisite in that Tabitha swore every nerve in her body was awakening to sensations she'd never even dreamed of!

Then she heard Brenton gasp. "What the?"

He was helpless as the walls seemed to stretch outward and the ancient runes became half-people, half-animals, watching their coupling, urging them on. Brenton's eyes widened as Tabitha tried to communicate but she was being ridden by an unseen creature and jerked like a puppet. Brenton's cock still thrust urgently but neither of them could come. The cock in Tabitha's ass seemed to contract and expand with a will of its own, then without warning it withdrew and there was the coolness of air on her backside.

Brenton and Tabitha were propelled to the floor, Tabitha pinned under Brenton. He rode her urgently, screaming, seeming insane with unspent lust and the hallucinations he must have thought he was experiencing.

From beneath him Tabitha saw a shadow moving behind Brenton, slowly like a panther about to pounce. The shadow was in the shape of an ancient Felidaen and Tabitha was helpless to warn Brenton. But if the shadow meant harm it was not of a visual nature as it absorbed itself into Brenton's body. The candles in their niches flickered and went out, plunging the windowless room in darkness. A single candle re-lit itself eerily and floated about the room bathing the straining couple in its glow.

Tabitha watched the surge of energy radiate through her lover. His eyes glowed like crystals regenerated and his cock swelled within her, opening her passage to a new feeling. There was a vibration through both their bodies as the room swirled. Their straining bodies lifted off the floor and levitated in the air, rising higher, until they were even with the height of the raised bed.

They were carefully deposited on the bed just as Brenton climaxed and shot a hot jet of come inside Tabitha. She clasped her legs around him and tightened her muscles. Instantly she screamed in relief as an acute orgasm rocketed through her. Exhausted and panting the couple clung to each other in a daze.

Brenton rolled off her, but his eyes still were a lighter blue and gleamed roguishly. "Did I please you?" The cadence of his low, deep voice was absent and in its place was a heavy Scottish brogue.

"Brenton? Is that you?" Tabitha wasn't sure if he was playing a trick in retribution, but how could his eyes change color? No, now they were his usual dark blue hue and his voice held no accent. Maybe she had imagined the shadow, but she knew she hadn't.

"Of course. It's me. What the hell just happened? This room, it's…" His eyes lightened and the heavy brogue resurfaced. "Aye. This is a fine body and I did pleasure ye, eh lass? We both did." He chuckled richly. "Your lover will be more receptive to this day with my help. Pity I can't stay. But the laws of the ancient ones must be upheld. Now my pretty, you and your lover drink the dram of potion, ye fine Gran hath brought."

The delicate twisted champagne flutes glided through the air, held by unseen hands. They tilted towards Tabitha and Brenton's lips. He spoke, still in heavy Scots, "I will be leaving after he drinks this, but I thank ye, lass and the pleasure was all mine!" With a half-salute the stranger in Brenton drained the glass and Tabitha found her own flute tipped to her lips and she was forced to drink up.

Her last coherent thoughts were, "What did it all mean?" Then she saw a shadow split off from Brenton's sleeping form and move across the bed. A wet kiss was pressed on her lips and the shadow moved off to disappear into the wall, forming a single ancient spiral symbol. Then Tabitha fell into an exhausted drugged sleep.

* * * * *

She awoke to the sound of whispering and thought it was the room coming alive again. She shot up in bed, disturbing Brenton who awoke groggily and muttered, "Meggie, why do you always wake me when you leave?"

Tabitha growled in her throat. "Who the hell was Meggie? Argh! Men!" Brenton had no idea where he was. He thought he was at the penthouse after a cheap lay with blondie.

She heard the whispering again and glanced off the side of the bed. Seline stood, her eyes averted. Not that she could have seen much of the couple's naked bodies, resting up high as they were, but she had to be cautious. Grandmother had warned her, and Seline was a good girl. Unlike herself, Tabitha sighed then turned her discontent on Brenton. She shoved him...hard. "Brenton wake up! Grandmother wants to see us."

Brenton ignored her. Tabitha leaned over and sunk her teeth into his earlobe. Meggie, her ass!

Brenton howled and shot up in bed. Seline hastily retreated for the door, leaving two black robes at the foot of the dais. Brenton turned, seeing Tabitha and she swore his sleep-soaked eyes cleared instantly.

"Damn! I thought I was having a nightmare."

"Was her name Meggie?" Tabitha's eyes narrowed into slits of green.

"Meggie? What the hell does she have to do with any of this? I thought you…this…all of it was just a nightmare."

Tabitha's blood boiled at being called a nightmare. She'd fucked the man's brains out and he called her a derogatory term. The bastard! Then she blinked in realization. They were in heated battle and there was no lust! The draught had worked! "Get up Brenton. Grandmother wants us downstairs. Seline says now! I think we're cured. Do you feel anything?"

Brenton looked at her naked body, then at his half-erect cock, which hardened perceptively. "Yeah, but I can resist. So we're done?"

"Yeah, I guess so." She tried to keep the disappointment from her tone. There was nothing worse than a clingy, whiny feline.

Brenton climbed down from the dais and picked up the larger of the two robes. "There is something strange about this house, your grandmother, and sister. They think they're witches, don't they?"

"Not exactly." Tabitha had watched Brenton's backside retreating down the stairs of the dais and stifled a sigh of remorse. Despite the torrid sex, she still wanted him, potion or no potion. "They're just different, that's all."

"To each his own," Brenton stated matter-of-factly. "I just want to get the hell out of here and back to…" His voice tapered off.

"To what?" Tabitha nimbly started down the stairs. She felt wonderful after the deep sleep, vibrant and totally alive. But Brenton was not going to finish his sentence. He was still being secretive about the warehouse and the money. The money! She remembered the pilfered nine thousand. Should she give it to him? She reached for the other black robe Brenton held out to her. But in a flash he pulled it behind his back.

"I think I like you better naked." Brenton's eyes were a clear dark blue. It wasn't the potion talking.

Tabitha's heart skipped a beat. "What's Meggie to you?"

"Meggie? That's the second time her name has come up. Why?"

"You moaned her name in your sleep," Tabitha accused.

"That may be, but she never did to me what you have done, and I don't mean slipped me a bad potion." His hand reached out and traced a line from the hollow in Tabitha's throat to her breast and made circles, ever smaller until he stroked her nipple.

Tabitha moaned in her throat. "I can't believe after all the times we've fucked, you still can think about it."

"I feel great! Like I've slept for a week and gone without…" Brenton took his index finger and licked it then pushed it into her belly button and twirled it around.

Instantly a twinge traveled from her stomach to her cunt as if an electric circuit switch had been triggered. She reached to part Brenton's robe and saw his cock fully erect, standing at attention. She moved forward.

Seline's voice on the other side of the door came loud and clear. "Grandmother says, you have to come now or something bad will happen!"

Tabitha jerked back, afraid Seline would come in and see another taboo sight. "We'd better go. There must be something urgent." This time Brenton handed her the robe and she threw it on, belting it tightly.

Seline waited on the other side of the door. They followed her like an obedient flock along the hall and down the narrow back stairs into the kitchen. Pots and pans boiled on the stove and Brenton eyed the concoctions warily as if a toad might jump out at him.

"Relax." Tabitha smiled. "We ran out of eye of newt. Now we just scramble eggs and fry bacon here." The sound of bread popping out of the toaster made him jump visibly. "Good thing you don't have that gun, or you'd kill the toaster, eh, stud?"

Brenton did not appreciate her sarcasm, which was evident by the glare he turned on her. "Well, if you'll excuse me, I'll be on my way. We obviously are cured or whatever you call it."

He planned on just walking out and leaving her? Just like that? Tabitha couldn't believe it!

But she needn't have worried as her grandmother came in the room. "Sit down. Both of you. Have some breakfast."

Tabitha looked about, "Seline said we had to come immediately or something bad would happen. What is it, Grandmother?"

"Just your breakfast will get cold. Sit, child, and you, my granddaughter's chosen one." She smiled at having given the young ones a bad turn thinking their haste was postponing doom.

"Thanks, I don't have time." Brenton looked puzzled for a minute. "Where are my keys?"

Grandmother looked unconcerned as she carried frying pans to the table and loaded up the four plates set neatly on place mats, with bacon and scrambled eggs. "No doubt in your pants, upstairs, where you left them. But you won't need them."

"Why? Am I going to take a broom?" Brenton swiped back.

Grandmother chuckled. "Spunky aren't you? I like him, Tabitha. He's got stamina too, apparently."

"Grandmother!" Tabitha blushed red, embarrassed.

"Both of you, sit!" Grandmother placed the skillet back on the stove as Seline poured orange juice. "Now I know you must be thinking it's late in the day for breakfast, but we keep to a different clock here, young man."

Brenton looked disbelieving at the domestic scene unfolding in front of his eyes. All three women had taken their place at the table, just like any normal family about to sit down to a meal. "You don't understand. I have urgent business to attend to. A matter of life and death and…"

"And you step out of this house and come midnight, you will be the one to die a painful death," Grandmother replied, matter-of-factly.

"What?" Brenton looked uneasy. "What do you mean? You broke the spell, the curse…oh hell, whatever that was!"

"The sausage!" Seline howled as she jumped up for the stove. Brenton's ingrained gentlemanly habits took over and he reached it first and turned off the burner under the smoking pork.

Grandmother looked on approvingly. "I gave you the first treatment. It's a two-step therapy. Midnight is when the turning point comes. You have to be here for the finale or it is all in vain."

"You mean more…" Tabitha crunched a piece of bacon.

"If you are both together and don't complete the cure. If you are apart you both will have the mother of all sexual awakenings and perish. They don't call it the little death for nothing." She chucked at her play on words as she took a swallow of juice.

"What time is it?" Brenton found himself serving sausage links at the table. He could not explain why he did it, but it felt natural.

"In your time almost seven at night," Grandmother answered.

"I have just enough time to do what I need to," Brenton argued.

"Young man. Do you think I would risk my granddaughter's life by letting you leave and possibly not return in time?"

"Look," Brenton began. "I don't exactly believe all of this but whatever you think, you obviously have some basis for it, so no, I would not endanger Tabitha, unless it was imperative I go so…"

"You may go tomorrow. There are preparations to be attended to and we will need all the time we have. Now eat. You will need your strength for the unbinding." Grandmother looked up from her plate shrewdly, daring Brenton to challenge her authority.

Something in her eyes made Brenton take his seat and begin to eat. Tabitha knew the look and why he was powerless to refuse. Grandmother's will of magic was strong, too strong for a mere mortal human to combat.

Just like any normal family they ate their seven p.m. breakfast with the exception of the sound of soft purring coming from the table over the dessert of clotted cream.

* * * * *

After the meal, Tabitha and Brenton were instructed to bathe or shower, scrubbing themselves clean. The catch was they had to be separated until just before the midnight hour so Seline took Tabitha to her room and Grandmother showed Brenton where another bathroom was located.

The Octagonal chamber had to be purified and therefore remain empty until the time of reckoning. This was no great disappointment as Brenton was not about to set foot in that creepy chamber alone and no amount of teasing from Tabitha would have any effect on him. It was just as well his car keys were somewhere within and there was no fear he would try and leave unless he braved the ancient runes and symbols.

At eleven, both Tabitha and Brenton were seized with an unrelenting thirst but were warned they could not drink until served in ceremonial fashion. At half past the hour they were both escorted to the Octagonal chamber. Tabitha had been briefed on what she must do whether Brenton was compliant or not.

The threshold of the chamber was hung with hemlock and an olive branch. The walls, which had been filled with the symbols and runes, were bare and now the floor was covered with the ancient shapes, as if they had slid off the wall to lie dormant on the hardwood floor. The Celtic symbols now joined together, as did the Egyptian and Bodiccean. Each in their own formations as if ready to do battle against unseen forces.

Four candles burned far away from one another. Two black and two white. Each exuded its own fragrance. If one's nose were finicky it could single out the smells. The spice of one, the sweet odor burning from another. Acrid mint and lemony wax drifted now and then through the room, leaving a heavy layer blanketing the occupants.

First Brenton, then Tabitha, was offered a goblet of cool water to slake their thirsts. But Brenton refused to drink and Tabitha switched goblets with him before touching the ornate metal to her lips and drinking deep. Brenton's trust was lacking but his torrid thirst won out and he drank, draining the goblet. Grandmother led Tabitha to the Bodiccean formation signifying the ancient women's warrior blood in her and Brenton was led to the Celtic symbols, in honor of the feral race of ancient times. Brenton looked none too happy to stand near the black shapes, obviously unsure after his earlier experience. If he thought it odd the symbols were on the floor, he said nothing, and Tabitha wondered if he attributed their placement to Seline or her grandmother?

Grandmother posed each in a standing stance with their legs slightly apart. She indicated they were not to move by a staying motion of her hand. Tabitha knew the Octagonal chamber was for ceremonies but her apprenticeship had not taken her that far, so she was ignorant what to expect except in following her Gram's instructions. Tabitha noticed the Egyptian symbols were in the shape of a cat and remained aloof from the others, observing but not participating. She had no time to further wonder at this as Grandmother bowed to Brenton, then Tabitha, then approached the Egyptian formation. As she bowed Tabitha realized she was paying homage to the ancients.

Seline followed suit then the two women withdrew from the room and closed the door. Tabitha stood staring at Brenton when her eyes began to grow heavy and her head sagged until her chin touched her breast. She fought the urge to lie down on the floor and go to sleep. Her head bobbed up and she saw Brenton too was dozing off. The water had not tasted strange but no doubt it had been drugged as part of the ritual.

They both stood as statues and Tabitha realized that's exactly what she felt like…stone. Her legs were locked in place and she could not move them. She wanted to drift off into sleep badly but she could not move and fought, her eyes opening and closing but unable to move any other muscle.

From Brenton's rigid stance across the way, he too was paralyzed and only his eyes moved as he tried to stay awake and stared across at Tabitha. He worked his mouth but no sound came out. Tabitha knew their vocal cords were useless.

Then to her surprise she saw the Celtic symbols around Brenton quiver and move. She tried to glance down as she saw a movement from the corner of her eye but her neck muscles were rigid and she only had a vague sense of movement at her feet.

Across from her the ancient Celtic runes began to elongate into shapes, moving as shadows of their former bodies. They grew until they were life-size with arms and legs but no definition of features, merely black shadowy forms performing their ritualistic duties. There came a whispering from the Egyptian symbols as they too shivered and transformed, but they had shadowy tails and ear-like protrusions from their darkened heads as they divided their numbers, half to attend Tabitha and half Brenton.

Tabitha watched as shaded hands removed Brenton's robe and wondered what he felt? She had not long to ponder as her own robe slid from her body and a blast of cool air hit her bare skin. She could feel but not move! They were virtually at the mercy of these strange creatures whose motives were unknown. Her feet were lifted and moved further apart. The shadows could move her limbs as they willed and Tabitha was helpless not to respond.

She watched as her Bodicceans and Egyptians moved away from her leaving her unattended and alone. Their shapes were womanly curves, lacking definition of feature. Likewise Brenton's Celts and Egyptians moved away, their size and width indicating men. Their ebony legs heavily outlined with muscle. Like shadowy soldiers each camp marched towards each other then passed, the factions switching human partners.

To Tabitha's horror hands nudged her thighs apart. The shadow creatures could do as they would and neither she nor Brenton could do a damned thing about it! Tabitha opened her mouth to scream but though her voice wrapped around the action, no sound came out.

Chapter Nine

There were hands all over her body; in her hair, on her neck and shoulders. Rubbing and manipulating her skin. She looked across and likewise shadows were all over Brenton, caressing, stroking. In their hands were tiny bottles of colored oil, which they deluged over their pores and worked into their skin.

Hands were on Tabitha's breasts and she could just witness edges of fingertips coating her orbs with a greenish oil that smelled of summer leaves and the fresh mown hay of spring. Thick liquid ran down her stomach and into her belly button where it swirled, filled and ran in rivulets. The lines seeped into every indentation on her body, tickling as it oozed into her pubic hair and delved into the top of her slit. Other hands poured globs over her back and let it run into the moon of her crack. Then the hands, large manly hands, began their ministrations, smearing the goo until she was wallowing in oil.

Across from her, feminine hands worked their way over Brenton's head and chest. His hair was coated, then hands smoothed over his shoulders and pecs. Oil ran down and his abdomen and six-pack muscles glistened. The hands approached his groin area and Tabitha wished she could growl. Those hands on her Brenton? Ooh, if she could just get free!

The hands were on his penis, oiling it with red cinnamon globs that spiced up the air even in Tabitha's circle. She found the odor irksome after her fresh clean scented fragrance. The whispering grew into a buzz as Brenton's cock was lifted and his balls coated liberally. His organ remained tilted up in the air like a posable Gumby, thick and rigid. Tabitha could barely make out hands at his back, obviously massaging and pouring. She wondered if he felt the oil in his crack as she did, wanting to quiver and shimmy as it tickled but unable to move.

Then her soul trembled as large hands probed at her cunt, opening it and inserting oil within. A voice heavy with a Scottish accent murmured in her ear, "Aye lass, I am going to feel you again. It's been hundreds of years since I rode a woman until you and I will have you again before the moon sits high. We all will have you and you will know each of us together and separately, all at once."

Tabitha did not understand what the shadow meant and she pondered it as she saw the broad shadow kneel and part her nether lips. A thick sandpapery tongue lapped at her core, suckling her clit until a flood of juice ran from her and mixed with the oil. She wanted to cry out, to protest, but she was voiceless. The whispering was louder and her eyes darted to Brenton, pleading for him to understand.

But Brenton's eyes were filled with hatred. Was it directed towards Tabitha or the shape taking oral pleasure from her? It was impossible to tell but Tabitha saw a feminine shadow go down to her knees in front of Brenton's rigid form and take his cock into her mouth, greedily. Brenton's eyes narrowed and Tabitha sensed his helpless anger as the tongue within her brought her to an orgasm she could not show. A tear ran down her face and as if that were the signal, her tormentor rose. He palmed her cunt and gathered the mixture of her juices and oil in a fist.

The shadow kneeling in front of Brenton worked feverishly as if keeping with a schedule. Brenton's eyes closed in unbidden ecstasy and he came with a rush. The shadow rose keeping a hand on his cock and working it as a stream of jism spiced with the scent of cinnamon, shot forth. The shadow scooped up the liquid reverently.

The group of Bodicceans around Brenton moved as one and the Celts attending Tabitha did the same as the groups walked towards each other. Only the Egyptians stayed in place, guarding their flesh and blood treasures.

Two shadows outstretched their hands and the shiny oil and sexual juices dripped from between their fingers. It should have fallen to the floor but it held in one elongated drop from each hand forming a mold. The hands joined and the two molds melded into one... The red blended into the green and formed the shape of a cat with human features.

An Egyptian shadow stepped forth and reverently took the molded statue, holding it high overhead. As if given a signal the female Bodicceans and male Celts seemed to meld into each other as they began undulating and rubbing against one another in a sexual frenzy. It became apparent as they dropped to the floor thrusting their shadows into one another they were providing a shadowy orgy for the benefit of their captives.

Tabitha wouldn't have found the sight arousing as much as an oddity if it weren't for the sudden burning taking place within her body from the outside in. It was as if the oil was eating its way inside her, passing through her skin to her organs making them pulse and palpate like separate entities. She found her legs free and her torso twisted in response to her agony. A noise across from her showed her Brenton in similar duress and able to move.

The Egyptians guarding him forced him to his knees, likewise Tabitha's demanded she kneel.

The Bodiccean and Celts stopped their copulating shadow show and lined up side by side. A Celt approached Brenton from behind, as did a Bodiccean with Tabitha. Tabitha saw the Celt part Brenton's ass cheeks then he seemed to meld into Brenton disappearing within. With the rush of cold air between her own cheeks something entered her from behind and pushed its way within. It undulated dark and cold, elongated, yet pulsing with energy. The internal burning stopped and it became almost pleasurable as one after the other the Celts and Bodicceans melded into the couple, until all that were left were the Egyptian guards holding the cat mold aloft and whispering ancient words that sounded more like the wind rustling through trees.

Tabitha was allowed to rise to her feet. She felt fabulous! So powerful and full of energy, nearly omnipotent. It was as if she was full of life force and could conquer anything!

Brenton was on his feet; the oil on his body glowed, outlining him in red. Tabitha looked at her hands and noted they were glowing green. Something else pulsed within her. She was an army of women warriors, their hearts pumping with hers, their words an ancient tongue spilling from her mouth. "We are the Bodicceans, a proud race of women warriors, refusing to be conquered!"

Brenton's eyes widened but they changed to a light blue and the noise from his throat was a harsh brogue. "Aye, as we the Celts give way to no man...or woman."

Tabitha was powerless to stop her answer; "Come let us anoint the ceremonial bed with the essence of man and woman. Then the contest of wills will begin until the

Felidaen and human are joined to break the bond as it is written. The ceremony will commence now."

Tabitha's arm reached out of its own volition and grasped Brenton's hand. Together they ascended the dais to the bed. An Egyptian shadow placed the cat mold on the mattress where it melted instantly. The green and red puddle spread until it covered the entire mattress and gave off a heat that hissed and sizzled and emitted a steam vapor. As Tabitha lay back the soft mass formed to her body, cradling it.

Brenton's body followed suit and reclined next to her as if following a script it knew by heart. Tabitha's hand gracefully arced in the air and reached to idly stroke Brenton's penis, passing her thumb over the tip until it bloomed full and hard. The urge in Tabitha forced her to roll onto Brenton straddling him just below his erect manhood. Her words were strange to her ears. "The Bodicceans always ride astride. Agreeable?"

"Aye. For now." The guttural brogue was raspy. The vapors from the mattress formed a cloud that mingled with the heavy candle scents and the oil on their bodies. It was if their bodies were separate from their minds and obeyed a stronger force.

Tabitha lifted herself forward and the tip of Brenton's cock nudged into her opening. The reaction was instantaneous as a flood of intimate juice slid over the tip. The cinnamon-like oil on his shaft met the oil of spring inside Tabitha, causing a chain reaction. Brenton's cock expanded, seeking its way inside her moist depths. A magnetic pull she could not fight compelled Tabitha to plunge Brenton's rod all the way to the hilt, until his balls rested against her. But she found urgency was not in the rune's plans as nature took its course.

The entrance of his cock made a sucking sound as the two thick oils slowed the impetus until the phallus virtually undulated sluggishly inside her, like a snake that had recently feasted and was too large girth-wise to fit into its hole and must work it way in. Tabitha practically hissed with impatience as Brenton's cock mocked her passionate embrace and took its time.

No matter how she gyrated there was no hurrying the process as the phallus slowed even more. It was as if the two oils were battling, hardening against the intrusion, forming a barrier to prohibit copulation.

In the back of her mind Tabitha's own brain forced Grandmother's words to the forefront. *"No matter what. You must make him accept you one last time. He will fight against it. You must be the stronger of the two. Once it is complete, then beware the other forces."*

The cock within her stopped moving as if cemented into place. The oil was binding them, making it impossible for them to move. Tabitha panicked. Grandmother had not mentioned this. Was it the way of the spell, or was it part of the ancient curse to be fought? Brenton stirred beneath her and tried to lift her off. No! He was coming out of her. Apparently, he could withdraw but not breach her completely. This was not supposed to happen!

The ancient warriors inside her whispered in discontent. "You must force him. Force him! Copulation is mandatory or you will both be doomed! Whatever the cost mount him and make him accept you."

Brenton was beginning to struggle. Whatever power drove him was equally as uncomfortable with the position and wanted to be free of her. His cock slipped out of her and though rigid, was covered in the red oil, hardened into an angry erection. He attempted to roll her off, but

Tabitha was aided by a power from deep within that allowed her to grab his wrist and bring it over his head. The bed frame was ornately carved with a heavy oaken headboard with holes cut in it. An unknown voice whispered to her to force his hand through the slot! *"If there is truly love in the heart, you will find a way."*

It took all of Tabitha's weight to keep Brenton under control as she obeyed and slid his resisting hand through the bed frame. Instantly, the hand was seized by a black shadow with the shape of an Egyptian headdress and locked into place. The other wrist followed, leaving Tabitha free to crawl down Brenton's body. He tried to buck her off but she clung like a vine, forcing his legs to splay. Helpful Egyptian shadows intent on fulfilling their prophecy grasped his ankles and held them.

The forces in Tabitha sighed and caused her to stretch with their power. He was theirs to do as they would. The warriors within him as helpless as the human. Tabitha crawled on her knees between his legs and took the reddened cock between her lips. The spicy taste of cinnamon burned the delicate tissue of her soft mouth as she took the tip and licked delicately.

Brenton muttered in an ancient tongue that spoke curses and ended with an English plea, "God, stop Tabitha. I can't take it!"

Tabitha answered back in a foreign tongue then voraciously began to suck the cock as if she couldn't get enough. There were a half dozen tongues licking him, cleaning him, but only Tabitha's lips and mouth on him. How could it be? The others seemed to goad Tabitha to continue. It was almost midnight. It had to be done by the lunar equinox or it would be too late! Grandmother had warned the consequences of the spell failing were dire.

Tabitha let the stiff rod fall from her mouth. It was ramrod straight but pink and clean. Brenton seemed more relaxed but that would not last. Tabitha made her way up his body and straddled his upper chest. The oil must be cleansed from her as well.

"Brenton, you must make me dispel the oil that prevents our joining or it will all be in vain. No matter what I say you must do it." She nodded to the shadowed hands that lifted her over Brenton's head and held her wrists and ankles prone as she was splayed over his mouth. Brenton's tongue whorled around the lips of her cunt, more curious than with a single-minded mission. At first it was a mere sampling, then as a man dying of thirst he thrust his tongue within and tasted her avidly. The sound of slurping and gulping could plainly be heard in the intense atmosphere and Tabitha swore there were multiple tongues inside her siphoning the oily juices. The warriors inhabiting Brenton's body were joining in the feast and relishing the task.

The oil within burned against her textured walls and the tongues were as ice to her raging inferno. She cried out as more oil poured from her passage searing her, but the tongues lapped it quickly and in its path came cool relief. Her clit was sucked and milked until she sagged against her bonds, wrung out and unable to give anymore. But she hadn't come. Dear God, how much more could she stand without release?

When she thought she would pass out, the shadows lifted her.

Voices whispered in her ear. *"It is time! Mount him and possess him… When you both have exchanged body fluids then it will be done. The potion will be absolved and the lust spell broken."*

Tabitha didn't think she had the strength left but the Bodicceans called to her and gave their strength to her tired body. She sat poised between Brenton's legs; his hands still held prisoner. His shaft was erect, reenergize by his own spirits.

Tabitha lifted herself to him. Suddenly Brenton lunged forward, breaking free of his bonds. Startled Tabitha hesitated and her advantage was lost. Brenton's voice was half his, the other half gruff and with a brogue. "'Tis not right for a man to let the lady have the seat twice in one night."

Tabitha was flipped on her back. Her warriors cried out at the outrage, but Brenton was too strong and held her down as his cock parted her labia and surged within. This time it slid deep, pumping with the strength of the men who inhabited his body. It surged with a force that rocked Tabitha as the Bodicceans within her were assuaged of their centuries of abstinence.

The pummeling staff worked inside her furiously, prodding against her womb and causing Tabitha to gasp out. It felt sinful to have so much pleasure as her emotions were torn every which way by the spirits, as one after the other they took their turn with Brenton, each segregating the feeling of his cock, using Tabitha for their vessel.

Brenton's body showed no signs of relenting as he grabbed Tabitha's ass and shoved deeper. He changed angles so her clit received maximum contact as he heaved into her, working her to and fro, bringing her to the edge. His eyes, a myriad of blues, searched hers as the spiraling in her cunt radiated into her stomach and she screamed as an orgasm shot through her and a flood of her juice began to slide from deep inside. As if the signal was given, Brenton uttered a guttural cry and shot his load deep, mingling with her own fluid. He collapsed on top of her, his cock soaking inside her, absorbing enough of her to absolve the spell.

Tabitha lay, her eyes open, watching the smile of pure pleasure on Brenton's face. Then to her amazement, shadows separated from his body and slid off the bed as the Celts having fulfilled their part, joined the Egyptians on the sidelines. Tabitha had the impression her own body was splitting as her energy ebbed and Bodicceans poured out of her, joining the other shadows. Together as one force they melded into the walls and became inanimate runes and symbols again.

As Brenton's breath slowed and his rapid pulse stopped pounding against her, Tabitha reached and stroked his cheek gently. He looked like a boy who had consumed the candy shop and it was all Brenton. No spell, no spirits. Just she and Brenton. He shifted his weight and pulled out of her but he made no move to rise. Instead he wrapped his arms around Tabitha and pulled her to him, spooning her against him as they both fell into an exhausted sleep.

* * * * *

Tabitha woke feeling like the cat that had swallowed the canary. She was refreshed and happy and...alone. What the? The bed next to her was empty. No sound came from the adjoining bathroom. The symbols and runes on the walls were ominously silent and still as if they'd never moved. And maybe they hadn't, Tabitha realized. The bed itself was as clean as if it had never been used for a ritualistic cleansing ceremony. The potions Grandmother had administered were strong hallucinogens. There was no telling what she and Brenton had experienced versus imagined. Damn, where was he?

She tumbled out of the bed as a thought poked at her mind. He'd been in a hurry to leave yesterday but had been persuaded to stay. But now there were no bonds, physical or mental to hold him. And whatever he was into at that warehouse involved guns and danger. Why hadn't he wakened her to demand the money she'd filched from Diamond Charlie? Why had he just taken off?

The black robe she'd worn yesterday was gone, but a set of clothes had been laid out for her at the foot of the bed. From the looks of the white cotton shirt and drawstring-waist navy pants, Seline had sacrificed some of her own wardrobe for Tabitha's use. Tabitha jumped in the shower, the pungent aroma of her and Brenton's lovemaking assailing her nostrils as the hot water sluiced off her body, leaving her clean but not any happier. She wriggled into the pants provided, which were long, as Seline was taller than her sister was, but Tabitha merely cuffed the garment by rolling up the legs a few turns. Heaven only knew where the clothes were she had arrived at the house with. But her tennis shoes were lying at the foot of the dais so she slipped them on sockless and scrambled from the room, hoping she wasn't too late.

As she ran down the stairs she fluffed out her wet hair, ignoring the constant drips of water that soaked the cotton shirt. Ooh, she hated being wet, but there was no time to groom her coat, or hair. She made the best of the situation by remembering Brenton's body snuggled to hers during the night and the satisfied purring she had kept low in her throat so as not to wake him.

She skidded into the kitchen where a half-filled pot of coffee brewed in the coffeemaker. She was wet and hungry, two worst case scenarios for a feline, but Brenton's safety was uppermost in her mind as she shouted, "Seline, where are you?"

A dark form came from the pantry shifting in mid-stride. Tabitha found herself envious of Seline's grace in transforming on the move in one fluid motion. Tabitha always felt awkward during her change, like an inept ballet dancer, having to stop and gather herself for the next step.

Seline's nakedness was no issue, as she looked Tabitha over. "You glow. That sex stuff agrees with you."

"There's no time for that now, Seline. Besides, Grandmother would wash your mouth out with soap if she heard you even say that word! Did you see Brenton leave this morning?"

"No." Seline sighed, her straight black hair fell in a curtain to her waist hiding her breasts modestly. "But I heard the front door slam. I looked out and saw him jump into his car and roar out of here, like bats were after him."

"Damn! You should have hidden his clothes!"

"Gram said to give them back after I washed them. They shrunk in the wash though and were terribly wrinkled."

Tabitha smiled. It amused her to think of Brenton's expensive dry-clean designer clothes going through the wash. "I should have thought to hide his keys, but damn, last night I wasn't thinking straight."

"It's understandable." Grandmother's voice carried from the kitchen doorway. "You couldn't have prevented his going anyway. The urge to go was stronger than my spell to stay today and without the potion's effect in binding him to you, he was determined to leave. Must be something urgent he had to attend, to streak out of here like that."

"Yes, well. That's why I have to go too. He's in danger; I can feel it in my Felidaen bones. Do you have the money I gave you, last time I was here, Gram?"

"Of course, child. You asked us to hold it in a safe place and we did. It's down in the cellar. Did you doubt us?"

Tabitha smiled sheepishly. "No, sorry. It's just I'm not thinking clearly still."

"But the potion has worn off."

"I know." Tabitha sighed, "It's just…"

"You care for the human?" Grandmother smiled knowingly.

"I'm afraid so." Tabitha groaned. "Why did I have to fall for one so unsuitable?"

"'Tis the way of the world." Grandmother laughed. "Go, child. Go to him and do what needs to be done. Let your instincts guide you. They will never steer you wrong if you truly believe in them. Seline, go get the money."

Seline left, padding softly for the cellar. Tabitha asked her Grandmother the question that had been haunting her. "Is Seline all right? I mean, her power, is it diminished?"

"She seems unaffected by the events of yesterday. I tested her on Spellspeak this morning and she can conjure and cant the necessary words with unadulterated power. She is almost ready to be initiated. It is well you are leaving though. Not to be harsh, dear, but trouble finds you and those around you. Some are catalysts for fate and you are one of those."

"I'm sorry, Grandmother. I will be out of your hair in a few moments. Can I borrow your car?"

"Oh, dear. I am sorry. It is not running. I use it so seldom, the battery is dead."

"I'll call a cab, then." Tabitha waited anxiously for the cab to arrive. She borrowed a handbag from Seline and put the nine thousand dollars into it. When the cab arrived she hugged both her relatives and promised to be careful. Grandmother's sense of humor surfaced again as she bade Tabitha, "Bring that nice young man of yours by again sometime."

Tabitha couldn't help smiling. She doubted wild horses could drag Brenton back to the Victorian mansion. She gave the cabby the address to the warehouse and he grudgingly agreed to take her the distance. She had him stop down the block out of sight of the Oriental Dragon's headquarters. When she got out her hand flew to her mouth. How the hell was she going to pay the cab fare? Damn!

She had little choice but to delve into the nine thousand. She would pay Brenton back, anyway. The cabby looked at the hundred she gave him like she'd lost her mind. He held it up to the light then screeched, "Get the hell out of my cab, lady! This bill is as phony as that hair color on your head!"

Tabitha's eyes narrowed.

The hundred dollar bill phony? No wonder Brenton wanted it back. She held the door of the cab open momentarily and looked at the bill the cabby threw back at her. Sure enough the "ghost" of Ben Franklin wasn't quite right.

The cabby threatened, "You pay proper money or I'll call the cops. I can't believe you think a cabby would fall for the oldest trick in the book, passing bad money! Why I have a mind…"

Tabitha patted her pants pockets helplessly. The sound of crisp money rustled under her hand. Inside the pocket she found a fifty-dollar bill. Thank God for Seline! She knew her sister's haphazard habits. Tabitha threw the fifty at the driver. "For your info this hair color is all mine. Now *you* get out of here!" She slammed the cab door, glad she hadn't tipped him more than a few dollars. Imagine him thinking her rich auburn hair was not natural. She grew it in this color and her coat was always shiny and well-groomed. Err! Men!

As she hurried towards the warehouse she pondered what this new info meant. If the money was counterfeit that explained everything and…nothing. It explained about the crates of merchandise coming in and going out. Undoubtedly the money was being smuggled out of the country inside cheap tourist items. But the money wasn't good enough to even pass as counterfeit and what was Brenton's part in all this?

This time Tabitha approached the warehouse directly from Old Harbor Road. The front door of the Oriental Dragon was unlocked. Tabitha didn't know if she should be relieved or further worried about what this careless oversight meant.

The inside of the warehouse was still dark, the daylight not able to penetrate its depths, causing giant shadows from the hulking furniture to be cast along the walls. Overall it was spooky and Tabitha wondered why she didn't notice the weird effects before. Probably too lust-intent, she smirked to herself as she negotiated between the furnishings. The wall panel was open and that further set her on her guard. But when she went through the wall into the warehouse next door the hair on the back of her neck prickled and her hackles raised. She smelled blood and a lot of it!

Chapter Ten

The warehouse was silent, eerily so. The bulky machinery was gone. Only a vacant space showed where it had stood twenty-four hours ago. Likewise the crates and boxes were absent. All that was left was an empty warehouse and a body.

Tabitha stared at the form lying on the hard cement flooring. It was pear-shaped and clad in a cheap polyester checkered suit. Blood pooled under the corpse and had spread in a puddle but the liquid had cooled and thickened and no longer ran. Thank God, it wasn't Brenton! Tabitha's heart thudded painfully in her chest as she breathed deep, careful to step around the congealed liquid as she covered her nose with her hand to keep from inhaling the strong metallic odor of plasma and the undertones of death. As if in mockery a fat, foul-smelling cigar lay next to the body, unlit but still odoriferous. A snub-nosed pistol was half-covered by the body, drawn but wedged partially beneath, as if ready to do business but too slow to respond before a shot was fired, taking down the culprit.

Her sensitive hearing picked up noises coming from the back office and it was easy to see the door above was open and light was shining weakly from the fluorescent bulbs. Whoever was up there had only turned on a few light panels, perhaps trying to keep a low-key presence.

Tabitha crept up the stairs and halted at the doorway. A scruffy-looking Brenton stood rifling through the room looking extremely annoyed. Tabitha watched him for a moment forgetting the circumstances downstairs. Brenton hadn't shaved and his clothes were uncharacteristically rumpled. Tabitha didn't care; she thought he looked wonderful and sexy. And best of all he was alive and from the looks of things, unhurt.

She must have made a sound or Brenton's instincts told him he was being watched, because he pivoted to face the door. He was unarmed but had a feral look in his blue eyes that spoke miles in the way of dangerous. Tabitha couldn't ever remember seeing that hardened look on his face, even when he had been raging angry with her.

His gaze softened, as he looked her over then groaned, "Tabitha, what the hell are you doing here? You have to get out of here! It's too dangerous."

"From the look of that body lying down there, I'd say so," Tabitha answered, still drinking in the sight of Brenton. What was wrong with her? Without the potion she still acted like a lovesick teenager with raging hormones.

Brenton ran a hand through his sandy-colored hair, also wildly untamed from lack of grooming. "That's Perry, *was* Perry. Muscle man and hired gun."

"And dead."

"I didn't kill him. He was dead when I got back here. No doubt he paid the price for trusting me and letting me get too close to the operation. By the time I got back everything had been cleaned out of the warehouse. I've got nothing. Months of hard work down the drain. Damn it! I've got nothing to show for this!" He seemed to remember who he was talking to and clamped his mouth shut.

"Brenton, what is going on? There's a dead man lying below and all you babble on about is danger and an empty warehouse. You're not saying anything I don't know. You have some explaining to do!"

"Not now, Tabitha. We have to get out of here. Or we'll both be keeping Perry company in hell."

"I'm not leaving until you explain about that nine thousand dollars that is plainly counterfeit, among other things!" Tabitha planted herself stubbornly in the doorway.

Brenton looked harassed. "I'll give you a short version, then we're getting out of here. Diamond Charlie stole the money from a bad batch and risked the whole operation by passing that money in the United States. It was never supposed to be circulated. There were near flawless bills being printed for shipping out of the country. Charlie was a fool to think he would get away with it."

"So you killed him?" Tabitha's soul wrenched with pain. Brenton was a counterfeiter and a killer!

"Tabitha, I didn't kill him. It was bound to happen though. He was mixed up with some bad company and doubling as a snitch for the government."

"Government? What are you Brenton, some kind of spy?"

"Something like that. Look, I'll explain on our way out. All the evidence has been cleared out, except for Perry, there's nothing left, and an ex-con killed in a warehouse isn't going to launch much of an investigation even with my word. Tabitha, do you know what your stunt with the potion cost?"

"I... What did it cost? Twenty-four hours of the best sex ever and I love, I mean..."

Brenton ignored her. "I have been undercover for two years getting cozy with the right people to infiltrate this racket. When I disappeared yesterday, it sent up flares of suspicion. They cleared out everything! They'll move operations to another city or country, and worse, they'll get away with it!"

"I'm sorry, Brenton. But if you'd been honest with me..."

"What? You wouldn't have drugged me? Imprisoned me in a sexual chamber where I don't even want to think about the strange things I thought I saw and experienced. Tabitha..." Brenton groaned in frustration. He changed his tactics. "Let's go."

Tabitha ignored him. "Is your name even Brenton Calder?"

"Special Agent Brenton Calder, FBI. My background is real, just tinkered with to make it look like I made a bundle on the Internet when it was a debutante media."

"You're not a self-made millionaire?"

Brenton laughed ironically. "On my salary? Not hardly."

"But the clothes, the car, the hotel."

"All owned and courtesy of the federal government as window dressing for my cover. As Brenton Calder, owner of the elite Arpel hotel, I am admitted into circles a regular agent can only dream of penetrating. Now can we go, my little curious one?"

She allowed him to take her arm and started down the staircase. "Did you say, *your* curious one? Then you don't hate me?"

"Hate you. I'm not sure if I want to strangle you for your little stunt or take you in my arms and try to recapture those feelings. God, it was absolutely intense and a damn turn-on! I get a hard…well, never mind. Now is not the time. I have to keep my mind on matters at hand but just smelling you, touching you, makes it damned near impossible."

Tabitha's heart soared. She clutched Brenton's arm in a half-kneading motion from her nails and a half-caress. Suddenly her hearing picked up the sound of footsteps. "Someone's coming!"

"I don't hear anything." Brenton sounded doubtful. They were only halfway down the stairs but then he must have sensed something as he propelled Tabitha back up. "Tabitha you stay behind the door. If it's who I think it is, then you duck out as I sidetrack their attention."

Tabitha tensed.

"Don't argue. It will cost you your life. I don't want to even think about that!"

"But Brenton, what about you? Won't they —"

"Shhh. I'll try and talk my way out of it. You go find a phone and call this number." He pushed a paper in her hand.

They were back in the office and Brenton pushed her behind the door as he walked across the room and stood by the long, empty table that had held heaps of money yesterday. His careless pose belied his tenseness, but from her hiding place Tabitha observed every muscle in his body was taut with anticipation.

It was only moments before a voice, deep and threatening came from the doorway. Tabitha held her breath as she glanced through the crack where the door was hinged.

"Well, well. The prodigal traitor returns. Any last words, Calder?"

"Listen, Mr. Lister. I can explain. It's not how it looks."

"Uh-huh. Let's see, you fail to return our nine thousand in bad bills. You take up with that little dish from hotel security, then you disappear for twenty-four hours, leaving the warehouse unattended. I have killed men for less. Look at Perry lying on a slab of cement downstairs. And all he did was fail to kill your little girlfriend. Now, I'm gonna put you on a similar slab, just as stone-cold dead, Mr. Millionaire Playboy."

Tabitha listened intently. Apparently Brenton's cover wasn't really blown. He was just being taught a lesson. Not that being threatened for dereliction of duty was any better than being found out for a government agent, but it sounded better anyway. Maybe they would go easy on him. How good was Brenton at talking? Tabitha remembered how he talked to her, in bed and out, just the timbre of his voice turning her on. Too bad this Lister fellow wasn't a woman.

As if reading her mind, a feminine voice reverberated across the room. "Now, Taos, don't be too hard on the fellow. He wanted a little pussy and obviously he wasn't getting enough from me."

"Now, Meggie…" Brenton began.

Meggie? Ooh, Tabitha wanted to rip the girl's blonde roots out. Meggie was part of this and obviously on the wrong side of justice.

"Shut up, both of you." The man known as Taos Lister yelled. "Meggie, you slut. I warned you not to get involved with one of my boys, no matter how much money he has. He's my bitch, just as you are. You want a piece of meat, girl? After I shoot your cheatin' boyfriend here, I'll give you a piece of meat. I'll fuck you over his dead corpse, then if I'm not satisfied, I'll put a bullet in you too."

"Now Taos, I know you told me only to get close to Brenton, but I wanted to make sure he was the real deal," Meggie wheedled. "You are my baby, my big baby and I love your big cock inside me. It does more than Calder's ever did. Honest. Would I lie to you, baby?"

"Yeah, you would, bitch." Lister's deep voice laughed. "But you're a good lay and I think I might keep you around to service me any time and anywhere. Yeah, that's it. Your penance is to be treated like the whore you are. Got it? Now you want to plead for your lover's life?"

"Hell, no. Shoot him and when I find that little redheaded tramp, I'll kill her too." Meggie's voice took on a hard edge. Apparently her good manners were a feeble veneer that had worn thin and cracked. When Tabitha had witnessed her in bed with Brenton before the potion, she had seemed a common prostitute, maybe that's what she was.

Brenton's laughter came from across the room. Only Tabitha's sensitive ears could pick out the brittle undertones. "Hey. Let's talk about it. Come in, have a seat. I can explain. There's no need to be uncivil. Meggie, I have no hard feelings, so why the vengeance? It's not like you were in love with me. Taos here sends you out to all his clients, isn't that right, Taos? Then our sweet Meggie keeps an eye on your clients. What better place to do it from, than bed? I guess we both used each other, didn't we, Meggie?"

"You're smart, Calder," Taos cackled. "You knew Meggie was a plant, did ya? Don't worry I'm not going to shoot your pretty little girlfriend for Meg's sake. I'm gonna shoot her for meddling in my business. No one takes what's mine, counterfeit or not. I taught Diamond Charlie that much, before he dove off that balcony, with my help. Now let's see. I'll shoot you with Perry's gun in the stomach. You'll bleed out even if someone does come to your aid. I shot Perry with the gun you left here yesterday. Perfect. It'll look like you and our ex-con Perry got in an argument and you shot him, but he got off a round before he died and gut-shot you."

Taos and Meg seemed to have no inclination to leave the doorway. Tabitha was stuck. She was going to witness Brenton's death if she didn't do something!

Brenton tried another tactic to draw the crowd from the doorway. "Come on Meg, how about a kiss for old time's sake? A last request of a dying man?"

"Fuck you!" Meg spat.

Taos Lister shifted his weight. He was an olive-skinned man, with slicked back hair and black snapping eyes, hard eyes that could kill without conscience. Tabitha saw them plainly from her position. Taos's deep voice belched out, "Now that might be something I would enjoy. Watching you and Meg getting it on. A sort of going-away present from you, Calder. I always liked Meg in those skin flicks she used to be in." Taos fondled himself through the dark wrinkled slacks he wore. "Never mind. I'm turned on just thinking about it. My dick is hard. Meggie, do your thing and suck me off. Killing always did make me horny."

"Now?" Meggie shrieked. "With him watching?"

"Yeah, now. Unless you want to join him and die together. Suck. Now!" he ordered.

Tabitha heard a zip noise then the sound of slurping. She wondered what Brenton thought watching his ex-girlfriend giving head to a two-bit hood who was going to kill him, unless Tabitha did something.

Taos began making grunting noises and moaned, "That's it Meg. Take it all in. Yeah baby, yeah." The sound of choking became apparent, as he must have shot his load down Meg's throat.

Tabitha knew the time was now or never. She transformed, sinking down with a slight thump.

Taos pivoted as she came out from behind the door, his flaccid dick flopping out of Meg's mouth. "What the...? It's a cat, a damned cat." The gun never wavered from Brenton as Taos turned back towards him. Brenton had no chance to do anything. It was all up to Tabitha as she crouched and sprang at the back of Meg's head. The blonde woman was still on her knees when Tabitha caught a hold of the teased hair and sank her claws in.

Meg screamed and jumped up, bumping into Taos in her panic. "It's attacking me! Get it off, get it off!" she screeched. Taos fumbled for the gun and tried to cover both the cat and Brenton, but Meg in her blind panic was running in circles, making it impossible to draw a bead on the cat, and worse, she was blocking his line of fire to Brenton.

Brenton wasted no time in launching himself across the room straight at Taos. He shoved Meg and her furry attacker, still attached, out the door and tackled Taos all in a matter of seconds.

Tabitha's last sight was of Brenton pummeling Taos with his fists to the floor triumphantly. Just at that moment Meg ran for the stairs and caught her heel on the top step. Both she and Tabitha tumbled down the flight to the landing.

Meg was out cold as Tabitha jumped off the prostrate woman's head and bounded back up the stairs. Brenton was sidetracked with securing his prisoner as Tabitha slipped behind the door and transformed. She quickly pulled on her clothes, and stepped into her shoes. She stepped out from her hiding place.

Brenton looked up at her in bewilderment. "Did you see that cat? It was the strangest thing, it just jumped on Meg's head and…well damn, I've never seen anything like it! Come on we have to get Meg under wraps before the Feds get here."

"She fell down the stairs. She's not going anywhere."

"How do you know that? You were behind the door."

"I…uh, heard her fall." Tabitha prevaricated. "I'm surprised you didn't hear her."

"In case you didn't notice I was preoccupied with this problem in a cheap suit."

"Yeah, nice job. I didn't know you knew karate."

"It's part of my training. I owe that cat a big debt. I wonder if I can find it and take it back to the hotel?"

Tabitha shrugged and caught her breath. It was now or never. "You can if you love me."

"What? Of course I love you. If I didn't I'd have strangled you with that stunt you pulled. Potion, my ass. When I get you back to the hotel I'm going to show you what I can really do in bed. That love potion has nothing on my natural abilities. You have anything to say to that?"

Tabitha uttered one loud word that came out more as a sound. "Meow." Then she transformed.

"Holy shit!" Brenton's blue eyes were huge as he watched the burgundy tabby cat change back into Tabitha.

"Welcome to my world, Brenton." Tabitha watched him, trying to gauge his reaction. "Now do *you* have anything to say to that?"

Brenton gave her that sexy half-smile. "Yeah, I think I'm gonna love being a cat person."

Epilogue

Tabitha snuggled deep into the warm comfy blankets of Brenton's bed. She stretched languorously. A deep voice next to her muttered sleepily. "Ready for round two?"

"Hmmm. In a minute. So none of this is the real Brenton Calder? The hotel, the fancy clothes?"

"You didn't really think I was such a clothes god, did you?" Brenton chuckled. "It's all part of my cover."

"You played the part well." She rose on her elbow and traced a fingertip down his chest.

"I still will, Tabitha. It's part of who I have become. Can you accept that?"

"Oh, yeah, but how will I know what is the real Brenton Calder and what is cover?" Tabitha questioned.

"Your hand is about two inches from a very real part of Brenton Calder. Besides, with your wacky family, I'd say we're about even on the cover-up scale. Unless you have any more secrets, you'd like to share?"

Tabitha grinned and cupped his cock in her hand, rubbing up and down. "Nope. I think that about covers it. Now I just want to become better acquainted with every square inch of you."

Brenton's arms lifted her on top of him. "Hmm, I can't wait."

Tabitha shivered as he sheathed himself deep inside her. They fit together like a glove. Brenton was everything she wanted in a mate and more. And she, well…if he had any problems with her species, he'd worked them out because he confided he loved the wee hours of the night, hearing Tabitha purring contentedly beside him.

But for now it was just she and Brenton melding into one. Touching and tasting, feeling every nuance of each other. Life was purrfect. Just as she plummeted over the edge of orgasm a fleeting thought went through Tabitha's mind. *I wonder how Brenton feels about kittens?*

* * * * *

Seline stared out the diamond-paned window of the Victorian Hill mansion. The full moon was rising, signaling the coven would soon meet. The air was chilly where it insinuated itself against the glass and found entrance through unsealed cracks in the molding. Even so, Seline rested her cheek against the cold pane, wishing she could go out just once and witness the coven's secret activities.

Heck, she just wanted to get out! It didn't matter where, just someplace outside, away from Gram's ever-watchful eyes. Oh, Seline loved her Gram, there was no doubt on that score. But she was young and restless, and wanted to experience what her sister experienced. Oh, not the luckless Felicia and her alley exploit that resulted in an unplanned nephew, but Tabitha's seat-of-the-pants choices, doing what she wanted, when she wanted. And that hunky Brenton! Seline sighed in undisguised envy. To experience that sex thing that Tabitha and Brenton had engaged in right before Seline's very own eyes. Wow! She grew hot from the inside out, just remembering the raw, passionate sight.

Seline leaned forward, bumping her forehead on the glazed pane. It rattled in the casing. This old house was getting positively ramshackle, Seline growled, then realized her thoughts. Even her words were old-fashioned. She had to get a life, live a little before it was too late. She groaned dramatically.

A deep voice behind her purred, "Why so glum, sis?"

Seline spun around. A pair of golden-green eyes glittered like sparkling jewels in the darkness. "Tom! What are you doing here?"

"Can't a brother visit his little sister?"

Seline narrowed her eyes thoughtfully, "On a full moon? What's wrong?"

"Nothing. Why do you ask?"

Seline knew Tom's proclivity for getting himself into scrapes, but something about his demeanor tonight was different, almost humble. "Oh, my Goddess! What did you do, Thomas?"

"I?" he chuckled. "Sure, I come to visit out of the goodness of my heart and you accuse me of ulterior motives. I'm hurt, sis…deeply wounded."

He stepped closer and Seline admired his sleek, good looks, so like her own, only lighter in hair color, like the rich shade of a Burmese cat's luxurious coat. He virtually radiated strength and vitality, and Seline envied his being born a male and able to wander at will. "How did you get here? Did you prowl?"

"Seline, relax. I'm a good boy and drove. See, fully dressed." He turned in an exaggerated pivot. He wore his dark jeans and sage-colored crew pullover effortlessly.

He knew he looked good and didn't care. Seline paid him no mind. He kept a sizeable wardrobe in one of the mansion's spare bedroom's closet and came and went as he saw fit. "So, why are you here, Tom?"

"For you, dear sweet, innocent Seline."

"Me? You know the rules, Tom. I can't go anywhere, or do anything on the night of the full moon. But someday…"

"Someday is now." Tom laughed heartily. "Rules were made to be broken. Come on, sis. Let's go dance by the light of the silvery moon, drink champagne and laugh the night away in careless abandon."

"Tom! Don't joke with me. I sorely feel the trials of following in Gram's footsteps on these nights, and here you are teasing me. You're cruel."

"I'm serious. Now put on something whimsical and naughty and let's go. Gram won't be back 'til the wee hours and we'll beat her back in plenty of time."

Seline's eyes brightened at the prospect before she quenched the glimmer as reality set in. "You know I'll diminish the power, Gram has trained me for inheriting."

Tom laughed loudly. "We're going out dancing, not getting laid. Jeez, sis, what kind of reprobate do you think I am?"

"I've heard…"

"Well, you can't believe everything you hear and besides, I wouldn't take you carousing with me, just a little wining and dining. But if you don't want to, just stay here in your crumbling ivory castle and pout."

Seline took all of fifteen seconds to decide. She spun on her heels and leapt nimbly into the air. "I wanna all right! I have years of living to crowd into this one night. Let me just grab some clothes. I think Tabitha left a few of her fun things here. Then lead on big brother, lead on!"

Tom looked startled at her sudden capitulation and had a moment of misgivings at her vehement declaration. What had he let himself in for?

* * * * *

Underneath the house from within deep chambers, leading hither and thither, there came a resonant rumbling and a keening sigh. It sounded as if the old house were settling for eternity. Above the creaking came a noise, like a whisper, escalating in pitch and unrest. It rose into a crescendo and filled the house, causing it to shiver in its foundation. The ancient ones knew their culture was fast approaching a crossroads where choices would have to be made. Choices that would change the world and either destroy their kind or allow them to evolve. The prophecy of Taharqa would not be denied.

Enjoy this excerpt from

The Phallus From Dallas

A Huge Problem
Mitch

Mitch stared at his huge cock. It was the bane of his existence.

Ever since he'd been old enough to get laid, women had run screaming from his monstrous organ. To make things worse, he'd gotten drunk one night and someone had dragged his sorry ass into a tattoo parlor. Written in gothic script, just under his navel, were the words "The Phallus from Dallas". The worst thing about that being, he lived in Austin. If the woman wasn't screaming at the size of him, she was rolling on the floor laughing at the tattoo. And the dark didn't help—the damn words were fluorescent.

If he ever got his hands around the neck of the bozo who'd hauled him into the tattoo parlor he'd... Hell. He'd been so drunk it was possible he'd done it to himself.

That would teach him to go out gambling and drinking. Sure, he'd won the championship. He'd deserved a bit of fun, so he'd gone out and gotten shit-faced drunk. He had a vague recollection of staggering around trying to pick up every gal he saw and being generally obnoxious. He'd acted like a jerk.

But to wake up with the most dreadful hangover of his life and the words "The Phallus from Dallas" written on his lower belly was terrible punishment. After that, he'd never touched another drop of liquor and promised he'd stay away from gambling. He'd sworn that on his knees, and in exchange, he'd prayed for a woman to call his own. Someone to love him and share with him all the joys and sorrows of life. He wanted a wife and a family, something better than just his two hands to warm his cock.

He looked once more at his colossal cock. There had to be someone out there who wouldn't scream and faint at the sight of it. Someone with a heart to love him, and a body to fit over his—

A nicker brought him back to reality. He reached over the bars of the corral and patted the shiny, red hide of his beautiful mare, Hi Ciarra. "Well, at least I have you," he told her, but his heart was heavy and he sighed. His daydreams were just that—dreams. He'd better get his mind back to tasks at hand. He had a long week ahead of him, and he had to get his farm in order.

Hannah

Hannah Hunt from Houston had a horrible headache as she headed her Honda towards the highway. She had a bit of a drive before she reached the Dallas-Fort Worth area and her destination, the Pro Bull Riding Association finals, but she didn't mind.

It would give her time to dream of that hunk of a man that kept her temperature hotter than the asphalt in the midday heat. She had memorized his face…tanned and lean, his square jaw marked with a sexy cleft, and that smile—lazy and knowing…as if he could be rode all night and put away wet and still come back for more. Hannah's fantasy and wet dream all rolled up in one.

Hailing from Austin, Mitch Winston was known as "The Phallus from Dallas" because when he'd won the Dallas-Fort Worth PBRA bull riding championship two years running, a rumor had started that he was hung like a

Brahma bull. The moniker had stuck, and every woman dreamed of sneaking a peek at the lusciously long cock that reportedly had to be shielded by a special cup for the bull riding event.

Hannah wanted more than a peek. She was obsessed with having Mitch ride her the way he clung to the back of those bulls. Only she wouldn't try and buck him off… No, siree, she'd lock her legs around Mitch Winston and feel every inch of that dick slide into her till he was wedged as tight as he'd go, and then she'd make him give her more. She'd clench her cunt around him till he creamed inside her, and still she'd milk him until he'd had the ride of his life.

Hannah had seen how the women buzzed around The Phallus as he exited the arena, like honeybees looking to pollinate. There was no doubt Mitch could have his pick of women but his fast and loose attitude wasn't fooling Hannah one little bit. She was the only woman for Mitch Winston and she'd make him see that!

Enjoy this excerpt from

Walk on the Wild Side

© Copyright Ciarra Sims 2005

Cathy Forester rubbed her tired eyes, as if trying to erase the sleepy droop that seemed to be a permanent part of her life. Her actions were observed and categorized as laziness.

Across the kitchen, sitting at the table, finishing his Grape Nuts, her husband Don set his orange juice glass down with a plunk. "Cathy, put the cat in and the dog out! Is that too hard for you to understand? Do I have to do everything myself around here?"

"Yes, dear." Cathy replied obediently.

"And why don't you join a health club? For heaven's sake, you are not the girl I married twenty years ago, but can't you at least make an effort?" Don gulped the last of his orange juice and adjusted his tie before grabbing his briefcase. "I'll be home late. Don't hold dinner."

"Yes, dear." Cathy finished rinsing the breakfast plates and putting them in the dishwasher. "Uh, Don?"

"What?" Don Forester looked at his plump wife in her worn pink chenille bathrobe with disgust.

"April down the street was saying how her husband Nick joined the Rocktree Country Club and his stress level was reduced to the point where they're like newlyweds again. And they have four kids. Why don't you accept Nick's invitation and go as a guest. Maybe it'll get that feather out of your ass before I take a skillet to your thick skull."

Don's eyes widened in shock. What had gotten into his normally docile, frumpy wife? She never spoke to him in that manner!

Cathy smiled sweetly, the easy-going expression on her face made her statement all the more unsettling. Don sputtered, "Nick's a pompous egotistical jerk. You know he actually volunteered to coach the little league team then put his own company's name on the back of their uniforms!"

"Yes, but he paid for the uniforms out of his own pocket. I know because when I tried to pay April for our Ricky's uniform, she wouldn't take the money. She said they get satisfaction from watching the kids have fun. Do you know how long since I got any satisfaction Don?"

"What? Are you insane? You bring our sex life up in the kitchen? This topic is forbidden outside of the bedroom and you know it!"

"Don, you are such a shmuck. April says Nick goes down on her at least twice a week. You know the last time you went down on me?"

"Cathy! Shut up! This is scandalous…"

"May 22, 1985. Yep, that's right Don. I wrote down the date. That's the last time you stuck your tongue in my pussy. What happened Don? You used to be Valentino in the bedroom, now you're Peewee Herman. It has to be dark and you have to be alone."

"Good lord, Cathy! I forbid you to talk to that April anymore! She has corrupted you! My God, you used to be a shy thing, the stolid mother of my three children, now you talk like a common whore!"

"What do you know about whores Don? Is that it, do you want me to talk dirty to you? Do you want me to get on my knees and suck your cock until you come in my mouth? Is that what you like these days?"

"Oh, my God! I'm going to go to work and call the health plan. I'll check our psychiatric coverage. That's it Cathy, we'll get you some help!"

"Up yours, Don. And I won't 'hold dinner' as you say. It's ladies night at the country club and April invited me as her guest. So stick that up your tight ass and smoke it!"

Don found his breath coming in short gasps. He was sure his face was mottled purplish-red and his chest felt tight. Was he having a heart attack? He had to get out of there before he exploded. Maybe Cathy's hormones were acting up. She was in her thirties after all. Female problems, his mother had called them. Oh, lord! This was all he needed when he had that big ad account on the burner. How could he laud Platinum's Prized Pickles without thinking of Cathy's lips fastened on a green gherkin sucking for all it was worth?

He rushed out the door. What had happened to that sweet, size five girl, he had pledged his love to twenty years ago? With each pound she had gained after the three kids, Don had found his libido waning. Now she was flabby and talked filth. Didn't a wife have an obligation to keep herself up for her man? True, Don no longer was a slim 34 waist, and his hair had receded to the point he needed some skill to comb it over, hiding the ever-widening bald-spot, but damn it, he was the bread earner! All he asked Cathy to do was bear his children, tend the house, and he'd bring home the bacon and dole out what he thought she should have. She was reneging on the deal! It was that April Smythe and her peacock proud husband Nick. They were a bad influence!

* * * * *

Cathy rinsed the last ceramic coffee mug with a sigh and rubbed her forehead where it throbbed after a morning of preparing lunches for the kids and listening to her husband Don's latest tirade. The kids had just left for school right before Don had started in on her.

April was right, Don was a wanker! It used to be all right. Their marriage wasn't an end-all passion, but whose was? Dr. Phil said one out of two marriages end in divorce and she and Don were still married, so they were beating the odds, but jeez… couldn't there be more?

April said Don didn't respect her and she was right. But Don hadn't respected her for a very long time and probably never would again. But April had explained, she and Nick had gone through a similar phase and they had worked it out with a little help. The key was, April said, that Cathy didn't respect herself and therefore others wouldn't either. Cathy had argued her extra weight was what made Don so upset and April being so slim didn't understand, but April had laughed, "You can buy this body from any plastic surgeon, but you can't buy self-respect."

Maybe April was right. After all, she and her yummy husband Nick seemed to be very happy, and Nick was to die for with his coaching the little league and always bringing April flowers. Damn, one day Cathy had gone down the block to April's for a chat and April had come to the door in a naughty outfit. Nick was home for lunch, she explained! The last time Don had come home for lunch was because he had diarrhea. Cathy was frustrated beyond belief. If it weren't for the kids, she'd have gone loony in this marriage long ago.

It wasn't as if Don had never been attentive. Back in the early days of their marriage he had bought her a dozen red roses every birthday and anniversary. Then one year it had dwindled down to an anemic one yellow rose. The following year a bouquet of daisies had been delivered a day late for her birthday… Then after that all she got was a card. Now it was a kiss on the cheek, and that was if she reminded him.

Cathy sighed, going to the country club with April would do her good if only to do something different.

About the author:

Ciarra Sims is a native of southern Cal. where she lives with her dogs, cats, and horses. She enjoys writing gothic horror, Regencies, westerns and contemporaries; but is game to try any new genre, whenever the notion pops into her head. She believes a person is only limited by their imagination and prides herself in following the beat of a different drummer.

Ciarra welcomes mail from readers. You can write to her c/o Ellora's Cave Publishing at 1056 Home Avenue, Akron OH 44310-3502.

Why an electronic book?

We live in the Information Age—an exciting time in the history of human civilization in which technology rules supreme and continues to progress in leaps and bounds every minute of every hour of every day. For a multitude of reasons, more and more avid literary fans are opting to purchase e-books instead of paperbacks. The question to those not yet initiated to the world of electronic reading is simply: *why?*

1. *Price.* An electronic title at Ellora's Cave Publishing runs anywhere from 40-75% less than the cover price of the <u>exact same title</u> in paperback format. Why? Cold mathematics. It is less expensive to publish an e-book than it is to publish a paperback, so the savings are passed along to the consumer.

2. *Space.* Running out of room to house your paperback books? That is one worry you will never have with electronic novels. For a low one-time cost, you can purchase a handheld computer designed specifically for e-reading purposes. Many e-readers are larger than the average handheld, giving you plenty of screen room. Better yet, hundreds of titles can be stored within your new library—a single microchip. (Please note that Ellora's Cave does not endorse any specific brands. You can check our website at www.ellorascave.com for customer recommendations we make available to new consumers.)

3. *Mobility.* Because your new library now consists of only a microchip, your entire cache of books can be taken with you wherever you go.

4. *Personal preferences are accounted for.* Are the words you are currently reading too small? Too large? Too...ANNOYING? Paperback books cannot be modified according to personal preferences, but e-books can.

5. *Innovation.* The way you read a book is not the only advancement the Information Age has gifted the literary community with. There is also the factor of what you can read. Ellora's Cave Publishing will be introducing a new line of interactive titles that are available in e-book format only.

6. *Instant gratification.* Is it the middle of the night and all the bookstores are closed? Are you tired of waiting days—sometimes weeks—for online and offline bookstores to ship the novels you bought? Ellora's Cave Publishing sells instantaneous downloads 24 hours a day, 7 days a week, 365 days a year. Our e-book delivery system is 100% automated, meaning your order is filled as soon as you pay for it.

Those are a few of the top reasons why electronic novels are displacing paperbacks for many an avid reader. As always, Ellora's Cave Publishing welcomes your questions and comments. We invite you to email us at service@ellorascave.com or write to us directly at: 1056 Home Avenue, Akron OH 44310-3502.

Discover for yourself why readers can't get enough of the multiple award-winning publisher Ellora's Cave. Whether you prefer e-books or paperbacks, be sure to visit EC on the web at www.ellorascave.com for an erotic reading experience that will leave you breathless.

www.ellorascave.com